PRAISE FOR AURORA ROSE REYNOLDS

"No other author can bring alpha perfection to each page as phenomenally as Aurora Rose Reynolds can. She's the queen of alphas!"

~Author CC Monroe

"Aurora Rose Reynolds makes you wish book boyfriends weren't just between the pages."

~Jenika Snow *USA Today* Bestselling Author

"Aurora Rose Reynolds writes stories that you lose yourself in. Every single one is literary gold."

~Jordan Marie *USA Today* Bestselling Author

"No one does the BOOM like Aurora Rose Reynolds"

~Author Brynne Asher

"With her yummy alphas and amazing heroines, Aurora Rose Reynolds never fails to bring the BOOM."

~Author Layla Frost

"Aurora Rose Reynolds alphas are what woman dream about."

~Author S. Van Horne

"When Aurora Rose Reynolds lowers the BOOM, there isn't a reader alive that can resist diving headfirst into the explosion she creates."

~Author Sarah O'Rourke

"Aurora Rose Reynolds was my introduction into Alpha men and I haven't looked back!"

~Author KL Donn

"Reynolds is a master at writing stories that suck you in and make you block out the world until you're done."

~Susan Stoker *NYT* Bestselling Author

When Aurora Rose Reynolds has a new story out, it's time for me to drop whatever I'm working on and dive into her world of outrageously alpha heroes and happily ever afters.

~Author Rochelle Paige

Aurora Rose leaves you yearning for more. Her characters stick with you long after you've finished the book.

~Author Elle Jefferson

Reynolds books are the perfect way to spend a weekend. Lost in her alpha males and endearing heorines.

~Author CP Smith

AN UNDERGROUND KINGS NOVEL

INFATUATION

Prologue

Justin

*H*EARING THE RATTLE of an old car and the sound of squeaky brakes, I press Pause on *Call of Duty* and get up from my couch to go to the window. I pull back the curtain just enough to see outside without drawing attention to myself.

It's dark out, but the light from the street lamp in the middle of the parking lot has cast a glow on the car beneath it. The rusty, beat up, powder-blue Buick needed to go to the junkyard a few years ago. The bumper is barely hanging on by the ropes someone tied around it. The back right taillight is covered in red tape that is peeling away, and I know from seeing the car in daylight that there is more rust on the car than there is paint.

As the driver side door opens, my heart starts to pound frantically against my ribcage, the same thing it does every time I'm able to catch a glimpse of her. My neighbor, the cute little blonde who moved in with Shelly, a woman who lives in my building. I've never talked to her before, but I've watched her more than is probably healthy.

I watch her get out of the car and grimace when she tries to push the door closed and it doesn't latch but swings right back open. "Jesus," I hiss when she takes a step back and kicks the door with so much force that the car rocks from side to side. As she blows a piece of her long blonde hair out of her face, it flutters in the light as she stops to rests her hands on her very round stomach. She looks about seven months pregnant, if not more. Then again, it could just be her petite size making her look further along.

When she finally starts toward the building, I wonder for the millionth time what her story is and how she became friends with Shelly. She looks and dresses nothing like the other women Shelly hangs out with. I've never seen her wearing makeup, and her clothes... well, her clothes leave everything to the imagination. They're baggy and do nothing to accentuate her figure.

As she gets closer, I notice the dark circles under her eyes and the exhaustion in her features. Every time I see her, she's either coming from or going to work. Okay, I should say I *think* she's going to and coming home from work. I've never actually spoken to her before, and she has no idea I even exist.

When she reaches her apartment door, she pauses and drops her chin to her chest. Even though she's in profile, I can see the annoyance and deflation on her face as she places her hand on the doorknob. And as she pushes in, allowing the loud music to stream outside, a roomful of people can be seen.

Seeing that, my fists clench. The urge to protect her, to do something, has me moving to my computer. Twenty minutes later, I go to the window and smile as ten people along with Shelly leave the apartment when the police show up.

Having done my part to take care of whoever she is, I go to the couch, sit down, put my headphones back on, and start up *Call of Duty* once more.

Chapter 1

Justin

$\mathcal{H}$EADING FOR MY Rover the next morning, I look to the left when I hear, "You stupid piece of crap. Open. Up. Now!" I spot my neighbor pushing and tugging on her car door, trying to pry it open.

I walk across the lot toward her then stand back, tucking my hands into the front pockets of my jeans and trying not to laugh at how adorable she looks yelling at her car. "Need some help?" I finally ask, taking pity.

Startled, she jumps back and her head flies in my direction.

I pull in a shocked breath when her eyes meet mine. I knew she was going to be beautiful up close, but I didn't realize how fucking gorgeous she is. Her blonde hair is up in some kind of bun on top of her head, drawing attention to her big blue eyes, soft, feminine face, and totally fucking kissable full lips.

"Um... no. No, thank you. I've got it." She waves me off, putting one foot on the car next to the door and pulling harder than she was before.

Knowing she's going to end up hurting herself, I get closer and remove her hand from the door handle. "Let me help," I tell her gently.

"Seriously, I almost had it."

I ignore her protest and move her out of the way then pull on the door, expecting it to open for me, but then feel like an ass when it doesn't budge. Pulling it again with more force than before, I shake my head when nothing happens. How fucking hard did she kick it closed last night? "It's stuck," I mutter more to myself than her, and she giggles. Turning to see her face, I watch her lick her lips and I fight back a groan.

"I may have shut it a little too hard last night," she whispers, ducking her head, but I want her eyes on me. I'm not done looking at her.

"What's your name?" Her eyes fly back up to meet mine, and I'm sure my question sounded like a demand mixed with a growl, but there's nothing I can do about it.

"Me?" She looks around like there might be some random person outside with us that she didn't notice before.

"Yeah, what's your name?" I smile.

"I don't know if I should tell you." She frowns at me, causing a little crease to form between her brows.

"You don't know if you should tell me your name?"

"I don't know you."

Chuckling, I move away from the door toward her then stop when her body gets visibly tight and her eyes fill with fear. My jaw tics and I feel my heart squeeze at her reaction. Pulling in a breath through my nose to calm myself down, I tell her softly, "My name's Justin. I live in apartment 210." I tilt my head toward the building behind us, hoping she'll feel more comfortable knowing I'm her neighbor.

"Justin." She swings her eyes from me to the building and back again.

"Justin," I confirm.

Licking her bottom lip, she takes a step toward me then stops and sticks out her hand. "I'm Aubrey. I live with Shelly."

"Nice to meet you, Aubrey." I take her hand in mine, realizing how delicate and fragile she is. She's so damn tiny her head barely reaches the middle of my chest.

"You too." She pulls her hand from mine and takes a step back. "Shelly said you're nice."

That news is surprising. I've only spoken to Shelly a handful of times since she moved in. Then again, she probably thinks I'm nice because I don't call the cops on her every time she has a party, which is pretty much every damn night.

"Crap, I'm totally gonna be late to work," she says, looking at her

4

phone, and I notice it's the kind of phone you buy for twenty dollars, the kind I use as a throwaway when working cases and don't want anyone to be able to trace a call back to me.

"Have you tried your other doors?" I ask, and her cheeks get even darker as she presses her lips together and tucks her phone into her back pocket. "Your other doors don't work either," I guess from the look on her face.

"No, only the driver side door opens. The other doors were welded shut, because they kept opening on the fly while I was driving."

"Jesus." I run a hand over my head and look at the car. I don't think she'd approve of me taking her car to the junkyard where it belongs and buying her a new one. At least not yet anyway.

"I'm sure you have better things to do with your time than stand out here with me. I'll just go in and ask Shelly if I can use her triple-A. Hopefully they can send someone out who can pull the door open for me."

She starts to walk away, but I can't let her go.

"I can drop you at work."

She turns to look at me over her shoulder and smiles a smile that seems to make time come to a standstill. "That's really sweet, but—"

"Sweetheart," I cut her off. "It's gonna take at least twenty or more minutes for someone to show up, and you already said you're gonna be late for work." Looking at me then her car, I can tell she's torn. "I promise you'll be safe with me." I draw an X with my finger over my heart. "Scout's honor."

She turns around, studying me, and then tips her head to the side. "Were you a Boy Scout?"

"No," I tell her truthfully, and her lips lift into a gorgeous smile then she laughs once more. This time, the sound hits me right in my gut. "You can tell Shelly you're going with me and send her a picture of my license."

She blows out a breath then nods. "Okay."

"Okay?"

"Yeah, okay, if you're sure you don't mind."

"Not at all. My car's right over here." I lead her over to my Range

Rover that is parked on the other side of the lot, clicking the alarm off. I open the door for her, making sure she's settled before I slam it closed. Jogging around the back, I get in behind the wheel and feel myself relax.

"This is a nice car," she says, and I smile then press the button that starts it up.

"It was a gift from a friend of mine," I tell her, and her eyes get big.

"A gift?"

"Well, more of a bribe," I clarify. "My buddy in Hawaii tried to bribe me into coming to work for him with this car."

"You're in Tennessee," she points out softly, looking around the interior of the SUV.

"Didn't say I took the bribe."

"But you still have this car."

"Yep," I agree with a smile, backing out of my parking space.

"He didn't get mad that you kept his car and didn't accept his bribe?"

"Nah, he knew before he tried to bribe me that I wouldn't leave my job."

"Then why did he try?" she asks, sounding adorably confused.

Shrugging, I smile. "Why does anyone do anything?"

"Good point."

"Where do you work?" I question, stopping at the intersection that will lead us out of the apartment complex.

"I..." She pauses, and I look over at her and find her worrying her bottom lip. "Do you know Dolly's on West 21st ?" she asks quietly, and my head twitches. Dolly's is a strip club, one of the bigger ones in town.

Beating back the sudden annoyance, jealousy, and possessiveness zapping through every cell in my body, I jerk up my chin. "Yeah, I know it."

"I.... That's where I work."

Well that answered the question of how she knows Shelly, since Shelly works at that club and a few others around town.

My eyes drop to her round stomach. "You're pregnant," I point out the obvious, not that she's not beautiful, and not that some men don't get off on pregnant women. But I can't imagine her working at a club like that.

6

"I help with the books, and on the weekends, I do the girls' makeup and hair if it's slow. Johnny… Johnny, my boss, has been sweet about helping me out, especially when so many other people have turned me down," she murmurs.

Noticing her chin wobbling, my teeth grind together. "Please don't cry."

"I won't." She shakes her head. "I don't cry. I never cry." The tone of her voice puts me on edge, but when she turns her head and I see the broken look in her eyes, something in me snaps, and I vow in that moment to do everything in my power to protect her. Always.

I reach over and take her hand, and her body jolts from the contact.

"I'm okay." She tries to pull her hand free, but I don't let her go. Instead, I thread my fingers through hers.

"My statement was insensitive."

"It's okay," she whispers, staring at our hands.

"It's not, but it's sweet that you're telling me it is." I squeeze her fingers and she looks up at me. "Let me make it up to you. Have dinner with me tonight."

Her fingers convulse around mine and her eyes grow in surprise. But then they dull a moment later before she looks away and out the window. "I can't."

"Why not?"

"I don't have anything to wear to dinner." She pulls at the front of her baggie shirt before letting it fall back in place. I want to tell her it doesn't matter what she wears, but I know women. I know it will matter to her.

"I'll cook. We can have dinner at my place."

"You… you'll cook for me?" She looks me over.

"Okay, so I won't cook. I'll order in." I smile, and she laughs.

Her eyes drop to my mouth and her bottom lip goes between her teeth before she whispers, "Okay."

"Okay?" I ask just to confirm.

"Yes, okay."

Hearing that, I grin. "Cool." I don't let her hand go as I drive her across town, and surprisingly she doesn't try to pull away. When I reach the parking lot for Dolly's, I drive her around the back to the employee entrance.

"Thank you for the ride." She lets my hand go to take off her seatbelt.

"Do you want me to pick you up?"

"No, I'll just get a cab." She smiles, opening her door, and I wrap my fingers around her wrist to stop her before she can hop out. She turns to look at me.

"I'm not letting you take a cab when I can drive you. What time do you get off?"

"I'll be okay."

"Sweetheart, what time do you get off?" My tone leaves no room for argument.

She stares at me for a few seconds before letting out a huff that causes that ever-present piece of hair in her face to float up and drop back down.

"Normally, I get off at 5:00 p.m., but some days I get done at 4:30."

"I'll be here at 4:30 then." I let her go.

She slides out but stops to look at me before shutting the door. "Thanks for the ride."

I lift my chin and she smiles, shutting the door. I watch her until she's inside then take off out of the parking lot, heading to the gym before work.

Chapter 2

Justin

$\mathcal{M}$OVING FROM THE kitchen to the living room, I stop in my tracks, looking at Aubrey asleep on my couch with her head on the armrest, her feet tucked up near her ass, and her hand resting over her belly. Letting out a breath, I move to the couch and stand over her, watching her sleep.

When I picked her up from work, she looked tired but happy to see me. I knew she had to be exhausted, so when I got her to my place, I showed her around then told her to rest while I put in our order for Chinese food and returned a couple phone calls. Apparently, I took longer than I thought. I pull the blanket off the back of the couch and lay it over her then turn on the TV and lower the volume.

Hearing her whimper a few minutes later, I turn to look at her. Whatever she's dreaming about, it isn't good. Her body is writhing and her breathing is labored and choppy. "Aubrey." I reach out and touch her shoulder, and her foot swings out, kicking me in the stomach so hard I grunt.

"No!" she screams, scooting away from me, her eyes wide with fear.

"Jesus," I whisper, and her eyes focus on me and her hands cover her mouth.

"I'm so…. Oh, God, I'm so sorry." She whispers, "Did I hurt you?"

"No, are you okay?" I ask, and her face pales as she scoots farther away. "I'd never hurt you," I tell her, watching her hands clench into fists. "Never," I repeat.

"I need to go." She jumps off the couch.

"Sweetheart." I reach out to grab her, but she dodges my hand.

"I'm so sorry… so, so sorry." She grabs her sweatshirt, and before I can stop her, she's gone, slamming the door behind herself.

"Fuck." I rub my hands down my face then lean forward, wrapping my palm around the back of my neck. My eyes catch on her sneakers in front of my couch as someone knocks on the door. Hoping it's her, I get up to answer it, but when I swing the door open, disappointment settles in my gut. It's not her; it's our dinner. I quickly pay then drop the bag in the kitchen before picking up her shoes.

Knocking on Shelly's apartment door, I wait only a moment for it to open and am a little surprised when Aubrey pokes her head out.

"You forgot your shoes," I tell her quietly, holding them out to her.

"Thank you," she whispers, taking them and starting to shut the door as I hear them hit the floor with a thud.

"Your food is upstairs. Do you want me to bring it to you? Or you could come eat dinner with me."

"I… I'm not hungry," she says, looking up at me, and her stomach takes that moment to gurgle loudly. I raise a brow. "Okay, I'm hungry, but I…." Her cheeks get pink and I take a step closer to her, watching her eyes widen.

"Don't be embarrassed. One day, you can tell me about what happened, but right now, I'd just like it if you had dinner with me."

"Are you sure? After what happened, I—"

"Don't think about that," I cut her off. "Just come up and eat. Please."

Nodding, she steps out of her apartment and closes the door behind her, and I notice she slipped on a pair of flip-flops. I take her hand, leading her back up the stairs to my place, then settle her on the couch before going to the kitchen to grab the bags of food. When I return to the living room, I can tell she's still embarrassed about what happened, but I know there's nothing I can do about that right now. It's going to take time for her to realize she can trust me.

"Tell me a little about yourself," I say, handing her the food while setting a glass full of orange juice on the coffee table in front of her.

"There isn't much to tell." She shrugs.

"How long have you been here?" I ask, setting my feet on the coffee table, lounging back, and hoping if I'm relaxed, it will help her relax too.

"Just a few months," she says between bites. "I was just nine-weeks pregnant when I got here, and now I'm almost due." She rubs her hand over her stomach unconsciously.

"Where's the father?" I question quietly, and her bottom lip goes between her teeth as her eyes meet mine.

"Hopefully dead," she whispers, catching me off guard by the fierceness of that statement.

"Does he know about the baby?" I murmur, and her head shakes side to side.

Studying her for a moment, I see there is something there, something ugly, and it takes everything in me not to drag her to my lap and hold her while she tells me about it.

"Eat, baby," I mutter, nodding toward her bowl. "You can save that story for another day." Her chin wobbles as she nods. I turn up the volume on the television and sit back, pretending to watch the show on the TV but actually keeping an eye on her as she digs into her food.

"Thank you. That was delicious," she says, and I turn my head to look at her and smile as she sets her bowl on the coffee table.

"My mom tried to teach me to cook. It never worked out. If I wasn't able to eat out, I'd probably starve, since the only things I know how to make are mac-and-cheese, hotdogs, and eggs. I suck in the kitchen otherwise," I tell her, watching as she tucks her feet under her.

"My parents are Irish and they both love to cook. Thankfully, they shared their talent with me."

"Where are they now?"

"Vegas. Well, all of my family lives there—my mom and dad along with my brothers and a few cousins."

"You came to Tennessee alone?"

"Yeah, they didn't want me to keep my baby," she whispers, placing her hands over her stomach protectively. "I hate her dad, but she's half of me and innocent. I know it may sound crazy, but when I found out I was pregnant, I knew—regardless of how she was made—I loved her more than anything else in this world. And I'll never let anyone take her from me."

"You keep saying she. Are you having a girl?"

"Yeah." She smiles then reaches out and grabs my hand, pulling it to her stomach. Letting her lead the way, I watch her hand press down on mine and feel movement under her shirt as the baby moves around. Looking up at her, I feel my face go soft as I watch a beautiful smile spread across hers and her eyes light with excitement. Without thinking, I use my free hand to push a piece of hair behind her ear. Her sharp intake of breath has me leaning close enough to feel her exhale against my mouth.

"I really want to kiss you, Aubrey," I whisper, and her eyes close briefly before she leans forward, resting her lips against mine. I kiss her softly then pull away, sliding my hand behind her neck to drag her head forward so I can touch my mouth to her forehead.

"That was nice."

I shift back to look down at her. "Only nice?"

Her blue eyes fill with humor as she smiles up at me. "Better than nice."

"How much better?" I rub the pad of my thumb over her bottom lip, amazed by how soft it is.

She tilts her head to the side and taps her finger against her chin like she's thinking hard about my question before she answers. "I think it was the best first kiss I've ever had."

I like her answer, but I want more. "I think I should kiss you again, just so you're sure. You know… so you have something to compare it to."

"You do?" she asks with a smile. I nod, and she whispers against my lips, "Okay."

I softly brush my lips against hers. "What do you think now?"

It takes a moment for her lashes to flutter open and for her to focus on me. "I don't know. I think you should kiss me again."

"I like the way you think." I nibble her bottom lip then soothe it with

12

my tongue.

"Oh, that's nice," she says then giggles when her stomach moves between us.

I lean back and rest my hand on her belly. "Does she always move so much?"

"Yeah," she replies softly, and I look up at her. "Especially when she knows it's time for me to go to sleep." She scoots back on the couch. "I really should go."

Fuck, I don't want her to, but I know she's right. "I'll walk you downstairs."

"It's not a big deal. I can make it on my own." She slides her feet into her flip-flops.

"I'll walk you," I repeat, standing, and she eyes me for a moment before nodding once. I open the door for her to step out ahead of me then take her hand and walk her downstairs, leaving her at Shelly's door with one more kiss and fucking hating that she's not going to sleep where I can keep an eye on her.

Chapter 3

Aubrey

I STAND BACK to look at Stella, making sure the makeup I'm doing on her looks flawless. It took me a few months to get used to being backstage at a strip club. But now I don't even think about the girls who are mostly naked, primping in the mirrors, chatting about what's going on in their lives and which big spenders are in the crowd as they get ready for their turn on stage.

"Aubrey's gone and gotten herself a boyfriend!" Shelly announces as she walks in wearing nothing but sheer panties and glitter, and all the girls stop talking.

My cheeks flood with heat as they all turn and stare at me while Shelly plops down on her chair, swiveling around to fix her makeup before she goes out to work the floor. "Shelly!" I hiss.

She meets my eyes in the mirror and lifts her brows. "What?"

"I don't have a boyfriend."

"I call bullshit." She twirls back around and points her mascara in my direction while she taps her foot clad in five-inch clear heels. "A guy came out and worked on the doors of your car on Tuesday afternoon while you were here doing the books for Johnny. When I spoke to him about the bill, he said it was taken care of. Who else would've paid for something like that except a boyfriend?"

I tap my chest and argue, "Me. I could've paid to have my own car repaired."

"If you were going to take care of it, you wouldn't have put it off all this time. And you just said 'could've,' not that you did," Shelly points out.

Damn, I did say that.

"Shelly's got a point." Stella looks up at me as she nods in agreement. "My momma's always sayin' 'Ella baby, you need to find yourself a good guy to take care of things for you.'"

"My mom says that too," Shelly agrees.

"You sure you don't have a boyfriend you've been hidin' from us?" Stella asks.

"I don't have a boyfriend."

"Then who's been driving you to and from work, even after getting your car fixed for you?" Shelly asks with a smirk before she whirls back around to face her mirror.

"Oooh, girl. No way did you pay for those repairs if you haven't even been driving your car," Lana, another dancer, says and crosses her arms over her chest. "Are you gonna try to keep fooling us or are you gonna admit you got yourself a man?"

I look at all the women in the room, women who have been nothing but kind to me. I love them, but I know from past experience that they're like sharks in bloody water whenever they smell gossip in the air. I also know they aren't going to let this go until I spill my guts. "You guys have this all wrong. And plus, the driver side door on my car is better, but I wouldn't say it's totally fixed. It still sticks every once in a while, and the repair guy said the others are all lost causes, since they've been welded shut."

"You shouldn't be crawling over car seats and consoles in your condition anyway," Maria, the youngest dancer in the bunch, mutters, staring at my round belly with wide eyes. "Not when you're ready to pop any day now."

"Is that why the new boyfriend is still drivin' you around?" Stella asks. "If so, that's a good sign. Protective guys are hot, especially when they go all caveman."

"Oh, I love a caveman." Lana gets a faraway look in her eyes.

"Stella's right," Shelly agrees, catching my attention. "I know I haven't met him yet, but he already has my stamp of approval if he's looking out for you."

A blush creeps up my cheeks and my gaze drops to the floor.

"Girl." Stella grabs my hand. "That's a guilty look if I've ever seen one."

"Um. Well, it's just that Shelly's wrong. She definitely knows him, since he lives upstairs from our apartment," I admit softly.

I lift my head to see Shelly's eyes widen in surprise, and she shrieks, "Your new boyfriend is Justin? Holy fuck! How'd you get in there with the Viking hottie?"

"I… I don't know."

"You don't know?" She shakes her head, laughing. "He's barely said two words to me in all the time I've lived there. He's a nice guy, but I've always gotten the impression he isn't too happy about having me as a neighbor, which is strange as fuck, since most guys are more than happy to be anywhere near me."

Maria snorts, and Shelly glares at her, asking, "What? You don't think it's weird for a guy to not be interested in having all this"—she waves a hand at her body—"living right downstairs from him?"

My nose wrinkles at the idea of my Justin being attracted to Shelly. I know it's crazy for me to think of him as mine, since we only met a week ago and I'm about ready to pop out a baby, but I just can't help myself. My feelings for him are growing by leaps and bounds each and every day we spend together. I mean, I let him kiss me on day one, and now one week later, I can't imagine my life without him in it. He's become that important to me in such a short time. It's kind of scary, but not in a way where I'm afraid. More like an exciting scary.

"Nope. I don't think it's weird at all." Maria aims a smile my way. "I really like that the guy Aubrey is dating isn't interested in his stripper neighbor. It means he has a little class."

"Hey!" Shelly cries. "I'm classy."

"Quit tryin' to make this about you, Shelly. It's about Aubrey and her new boyfriend." Lana sighs.

"He's not really my boyfriend," I say for the hundredth time, even though I'm becoming a little confused about the status of our relationship. I'm not exactly sure how the whole relationship thing works, since I've never been in one before, but I'm pretty sure you aren't boyfriend and girlfriend until you have a conversation about it.

"Did he get your car fixed for you?" Stella asks.

"Yeah."

She looks up from doing the straps on her heels and raises an eyebrow at me. "And he's still drivin' you to work?"

"Uh-huh."

"He feedin' you too?"

Stella is one of my favorite dancers, but if she keeps up with this, she might lose her spot.

"Umm...."

"He better be," Shelly grumbles. "She hasn't been around enough to touch any of the food in our kitchen all week."

Stella's smile is blinding. "So he's been makin' sure you get breakfast, lunch, and dinner?"

Breakfast and dinner, mostly, I think but don't say. "Umm, we eat together, but he has work too."

"Mm-hmm," Maria hums. "He's spending all his free time with you and taking care of you while he's doing it. Definite boyfriend material!"

"Hold up!" Stella holds up a finger. "We skipped one important step in the boyfriend test. I know the baby is due any day now, but have you gotten physical with him? Even if it's just kissin'?"

"Don't you all have work to do?" I ask, knowing I'm now bright red.

"Oh, avoidance. It must have been good," Lana says.

"How was it?" Shelly asks.

I shrug one shoulder. "Amazing, even if I don't really have anything to compare it to," I reply quietly, and everyone's eyes drop to my round belly and the ripple of my shirt where my baby girl is kicking. I know these women have seen enough of the ugly side of the world to understand how I could be having a baby and never really been kissed.

"Oh, honey," Maria whispers, and my throat gets tight as she turns away to blot under her eyes with a tissue.

17

Watching her, I startle when Stella takes my hand, and my gaze meets hers for a moment before she squeezes my fingers then leaves the room and Lana does the same.

I take a seat in Stella's now empty chair and try to fight back the tears I feel creeping up my throat as I watch Shelly put the finishing touches on her makeup. "I know we're complete opposites and I haven't been the best roommate, but I'm damn proud to call you my friend. You deserve the best, and if Justin's gonna give that to you, he's got my stamp of approval," she says quietly.

Tears spill down my cheeks as she comes over and squeezes my shoulder before walking out of the dressing room to head out on stage for her set. I know Shelly and I will never be best friends, but I owe her a lot. Without her allowing me to live with her, I'm not sure where I would've ended up living. Finding a job would've been harder too, since she's the one who introduced me to Johnny. And I might never have met Justin, which would've been a tragedy, considering the way he makes me feel.

"Lover boy might have gotten the thumbs-up from Shelly and the rest of your girls, but I need to meet him before I can sign off on this relationship," Johnny says, and I spin my chair around to look at him as I wipe my cheeks.

I smile, thinking about how he'll react to Justin, whose nothing like I expected, not from just looking at him. And if Shelly hadn't told me he was nice, I'm not sure I would've been able to get up the nerve to accept that ride from him. Lucky for me, he's the kind of guy who won't mind being checked out by a brute and a bunch of dancers, if that's what it takes to make me happy. But that doesn't mean I'm in a rush to make it happen, at least not until I'm sure what's going on between the two of us.

Chapter 4

Justin

TWO WEEKS. TWO weeks of mornings and evenings with Aubrey, and every single one of them have left me feeling completely fucking unhinged. I want her more than my next breath and know from the look in her eyes when we talk or when I kiss her that she feels the same thing. I breathe deep, finishing my set of reps. Working out isn't helping like I thought it would. I have never been a gym rat, but with her, I'm turning into one. It's my outlet, my way of getting rid of the pent-up energy I'm now carrying around.

Drying off my face and chest, I pick up my cell and frown when I see she's called me more than once. If she's calling me over and over in the middle of the day, then something must be wrong. She's always careful about using her phone, since she's on a cheap prepaid plan with limited minutes. And so far, she's refused to let me buy her a new one or add her to my plan. The only reason I've let the argument slide is because she spends all her free time with me, so I haven't pushed the issue yet.

I call her back and my heart drops when she doesn't pick up. "Fuck," I grunt, shoving my shit into my bag and dragging my shirt on so I can head out to my Rover. After I toss my bag into the back seat, I climb behind the wheel. My cell rings, and seeing her name on the screen loosens some of the tension in my muscles as I answer, "Aubrey, baby, you okay?"

"No," she sniffles out in a small voice, and my heart drops again.

My need to get to her is even more urgent, hearing how scared she sounds. "Where are you?" I ask, starting my car.

"At my doctor's office," she replies, and I step on the gas, thinking about all the things that could possibly go wrong at this stage in her pregnancy. "Can you come pick me up? I can't get my stupid car to start."

She's usually okay with me driving her around, but this morning she insisted on taking her car to work. Now I get why. Last week, I took her to her appointment. She'd been embarrassed to change into a gown with me in the room, even with my back turned. And then there had been an awkward silence when the doctor had done the physical exam, and when I turned around, her cheeks and neck were the cutest pink color. For someone who is due to have a baby any day now, she seems so innocent, and that only makes me want her more.

"Where are you now?"

"Sitting in my car, praying to the gods it magically turns on."

I chuckle. "Leave the car and go back inside," I order, sensing this is the opportunity I was waiting for to get rid of the damn thing. "I'll have it towed and get it looked at."

"We both know I don't have the money to cover the tow, let alone what it will cost to fix my piece-of-crap car." I smile as she grumbles, because I know there isn't going to be a bill to fix it. And the only person who will be looking at it is the guy at the junkyard.

"Babe, go inside. I'm on my way, and I don't like the idea of you sitting in your car."

"Justin."

"Please, baby."

"I know it's wrong to accept your help on something this big, but I'm uncomfortable and just want to be home, cuddled up on the couch with you, a fuzzy blanket, and something to drink." I hear her pull in a breath. "It's already been a really long day, and I'm tired and thirsty."

As much as I wish she'd just stay with me at my apartment, she's still living with Shelly. But I feel like we're taking a step in the right direction with her calling my place her home, since it's for damn sure going to be where she lives as soon as I can talk her into it. And now that I know she already thinks of it that way, I'm shaving some time off of how long I'm willing to wait for that to happen.

"Go back inside the building and sit tight, sweetheart. I'll be there in less than ten minutes to pick you up, and then I'll take you home and get you whatever the fuck you want."

"Okay, Justin."

Her easy agreement reminds me how tired she is, and I step on the gas to cut down on how long it'll take me to get to her. At the first red light I hit, I send a quick text to Kenton's woman, Autumn, to ask her if she has time to run out and buy a few things for me and drop them off at my place. She's curious as fuck about why I need a fuzzy blanket and Aubrey's favorite tea but says she'll take care of it right away.

With that taken care of, I manage to make it across town in eight minutes, and as I pull onto the street where her doctor's office is, I can't help but think about how different it is from the neighborhood where Dolly's is located. I hate the idea of her working there, but we aren't at a place yet where I can insist she quit her job and let me take care of her. I've worked too hard to get close to her to fuck it up by being pushy. Or at least I keep reminding myself of that anytime the urge to chain her to my side gets too strong.

For now, I need to be satisfied with what she's willing to give. One of those things is normally letting me be her ride to and from work, since her car really is a piece of shit. It's a win-win for me, because I don't have to worry about her getting stuck on the side of the road somewhere, and it sends a reminder to everyone at the strip club that she's mine, even if she isn't ready to admit it yet.

A few days ago, when she let me drop her off, I pulled her boss Johnny aside and had a talk with him about keeping her safe while she's there. He knows I work for Kenton, and that alone would have been enough to get him to agree. But he surprised me when he turned that shit around on me and acted like a big brother as he grilled me about my intentions toward her. He wasn't what I was expecting at all. Once I made my place in her life crystal clear, he told me how relieved he was that Aubrey had someone in her life who gives a shit about her.

Giving a shit doesn't begin to describe how I feel when I pull up in front of the building and she walks outside. My heart belongs to the cute little blonde with the big baby belly making her way to my Rover. Leaving the engine running, I hop out and hurry around the front so I can open her door and help her up into the seat. Then I pull the seat belt around her, laughing when I feel her baby girl kick my hand. "It's almost like she knows I'm here and is saying hello."

Aubrey smiles up at me. "We spend so much time together; I wouldn't be surprised if she recognizes your voice."

"If she doesn't yet, she will soon," I promise as I shut the door and go back around to my side. I like the idea a fuck of a lot more than I'm willing to admit to her. I don't think she's ready to hear that I already feel as territorial about her daughter as I do her. I might not have been there when she was created, but the baby is more mine than the piece of shit who'd gotten Aubrey pregnant. The thought of how scared Aubrey sounded when she mentioned him has my hands clenching into fists. I take a deep breath to calm myself down before I climb into the SUV and pull away from the curb.

"You want me to stop and pick anything up on our way home?"

She lets out a deep sigh and rubs her belly. "A magic pill that will put me into labor?"

"Sorry, sweetheart. I don't think they carry those anywhere around here."

Folding her arms over her belly, she sighs again. "We should invent them. I bet we'd make millions off something like that."

Even with a frown on her beautiful face, she's so fucking cute I can't help but chuckle. "How good are you at chemistry?"

"Not good enough for something like that," she grumbles. "I only took it in high school, not college. My classes there were all pretty much focused on my accounting degree. It was the only way I could convince my brother to pay for it."

Her blue eyes go wide before her gaze darts to the window. She barely ever talks about her family, and whenever she lets something slip about them, she acts like she's waiting for me to grill her about them.

Instead, I ignore the mention of her brother and change the subject. When she's ready to share more, I'll be here to listen. "Then I guess we'll have to come up with some other idea to make our millions."

"It's not even the loss of money that disappoints me." She rubs her hands over belly. "It's just that I'm more than ready to give birth to my baby girl, but she seems to be happy staying right where she is."

"What did the doctor say?"

"I'm not technically overdue until I'm past the forty-two-week mark."

Thinking about her appointment last week, I ask, "You're forty weeks now, right?"

"Yup, today, as a matter of fact. It's supposed to be my due date." She looks down at her belly and adds, "Which means you're supposed to come out now."

"Only five percent of babies are born on their due date."

Her blonde hair spills over her shoulder as she tilts her head to the side. "How do you know that?"

I shift in my seat and shrug. "I looked it up online."

"I guess I should've asked; why do you know that?"

"Researching shit is kind of my thing." I run a hand through my hair as I stop at a red light then look at her. "And I figured it couldn't hurt if I knew more about pregnancies."

"Couldn't hurt, huh?" She quirks a brow at me, her lips tilting up at the edges. "You shouldn't try to play this down when it's super sweet that you went to all that effort for me."

"Looking up stuff about pregnancies online didn't take a whole lot of effort." I take her hand and brush my lips over her knuckles before setting it back down on her belly. *Compared to everything I want to do for you, it's barely a drop in the bucket,* I think but don't say. "There are a lot of reasons why it would be hard for the doctor to pinpoint when you're due."

"I know exactly when my baby was conceived."

I clench the steering wheel so hard my knuckles turn white. The thought of her with another guy sparks an irrational jealousy inside me. It's not like I don't have a past of my own or even that I think she wants to have anything to do with that asshole again. Especially not with the darkness I saw in her bright eyes the one time she mentioned him to me.

"Hey," she whispers, reaching out to stroke my arm as I pull into the parking lot at our apartment building. "The only good thing that came out of that night was my baby."

I want to ask for the whole story, but she's going to have the baby any day now and the last thing I want to do is cause her additional stress. "I'm sure it's hard to wait a little longer, since you were hoping to have her by today, but another two weeks is hardly any time at all," I say, even though I'm sure I have the longest case of blue balls in the history of blue balls.

"That's easy for you to say. You're not the one walking around looking like a beached whale."

"You're beautiful," I scold as I park then jump out. I help her down from her seat, and when her feet touch the ground, I move in. I cup her face with my palms and tilt her head back to stare into her eyes. "I'd probably go to hell for some of the things I want to do to you."

Her plump lips go round as she whispers, "Oh."

I claim her mouth in a deep kiss, and she has a dazed look in her eyes when I finally pull away. "But I figure burning in hell would be a small price to pay to have you."

Chapter 5

Aubrey

I WAKE FROM my dream, needy and a little breathless, feelings I've gotten used to since Justin and I shared our first kiss. Only now the desire is getting harder to deal with, especially when in my dreams we always share more than just a few innocent kisses.

I don't even want to open my eyes. I don't want to lose the last image I have in my mind of Justin and me together, but at the sound of low murmuring in the next room, I realize I'm not on Justin's couch anymore. I open my eyes and look around his room, having no idea how I ended up here. The last thing I remember before I fell asleep was him rubbing my feet after making me eat something.

I start to smile as contentment fills my chest, but that emotion is wiped away when I hear feminine laughter filter through the door, mixed with his deep chuckle. A surge of jealousy courses through me at the thought of him spending time with another woman. I know I don't have any right to feel that way, but that still doesn't stop me from rolling me and my big belly off his mattress.

I walk lightly to the closed door and try to listen to what's happening in the other room. When I don't hear more than quiet murmurings, I nudge it open, hoping I can sneak down the hallway a little without getting caught. I should know better than to even try to be stealthy, since he has a way of sensing me even when he's busy with something else. More than once he's been in the middle of an Xbox game with guns going off or working on his computer and still alert enough to hear my breath catch if my girl kicks too hard.

"Baby, what are you doing up already?" Before I have a chance to respond, I hear him murmur to his guest, "Don't leave yet. I'd like you to meet Aubrey."

"Are you kidding me? I don't care how big you're getting now that you're working out so much. You couldn't pry me out of here with a crowbar. Do you know how long I've been waiting to meet your mystery woman?"

Mystery woman? I can't help but smile at the description, since I'm the furthest thing from it. The only thing mysterious about me is what a hot guy like Justin is doing spending so much time with me. Well, that and the life I left behind in Vegas, but nobody in Tennessee knows anything about that.

I only make it a few steps down the hallway before Justin rounds the corner. With his blond hair, scruff-covered cheeks, crystal-blue eyes, and muscular build, he looks like he could take down an army without help. But I've felt nothing but safe in his strong arms and experienced nothing but gentleness when he's touched me.

"You okay?" he asks, and I realize I've been standing feet away staring at him.

"I heard voices," I say, and his expression softens.

"Sorry, baby. You fell asleep, so I moved you to the bedroom and tried to keep it down to a low roar out here so you could nap as long as you needed."

Now I know how I ended up in his bed, and I really wish I'd been awake for the experience of being tucked in by him.

"Autumn's here. She brought some stuff over for you."

"Autumn?" My brow wrinkles in confusion. Maybe it's pregnancy brain or just that I haven't woken all the way up from my nap, but I don't think I've ever heard of her.

"C'mon, she wants to meet you before she heads out." He comes toward me and takes my hand. I let him lead me into the living room where a stunning redhead is waiting for us. She's prettier than most of the showgirls at the big casinos in Vegas, and it makes me more self-conscious of my tousled hair, puffy eyes, huge baby belly, and swollen feet. She looks like the kind of woman Justin should date, not me. But she seems so excited to meet me that I smile back when she rushes forward to give me a hug.

"Oh my gosh! Look at you!" She slaps Justin's shoulder. "Why have you been keeping Aubrey a secret from all of us?"

Justin pulls me into his side and wraps an arm around my waist. "Look at her. Can you really blame me for wanting to keep her all to myself for as long as I can?"

"Not at all." She grins and pokes him in the abs. "Just don't expect me to be as tightlipped about her as you've been. Kenton's been wondering what's been distracting you lately, and I can't wait to brag about how I found out what it was before he did."

I don't quite understand what all Justin does for work, but I recognize his boss's name. "Do you work for Kenton too?"

"Nope, I'm a nurse." She lifts her left hand and flashes a sapphire-and-diamond ring with a matching band. "I'm married to Kenton."

"Oh!" I feel a big wave of relief as I grasp her connection to Justin. She's his boss's wife, and very happily taken, judging by the gleam in her eyes when she talks about her husband. "Justin talks about him a lot," I say.

"Should I be offended that you haven't talked about me a lot?"

"Sweetcheeks, don't fucking start."

"Sweetcheeks?" I echo softly, stiffening a little.

"It's a stupid nickname Justin came up with to mess with Kenton," Autumn explains with a roll of her eyes.

"He makes it too easy." Justin shakes his head then tips his head down to look at me. "The idiot knows she's like my sister."

"Again, I'm thinking I should be offended that you haven't talked about me," Autumn inserts, and I relax completely, listening to their banter and better understanding their relationship.

"Well, I better head out. I have a few more errands I need to run before I go home, and we both know Kenton will only be able to hold off calling me for so long, wondering when I'll be back." She gives us both a hug before walking to the door and turning to look at me over her shoulder. "I'd love to hang out together some time."

I pat my belly. "I'd love that, but it's hard for me to make plans right now, because my daughter is due any day now."

"You're having a girl?" She grins. "Is there anything you need? Or can I go crazy buying tiny, pink clothes for a baby gift?"

My cheeks fill with heat. "Oh! That wasn't a hint for gifts or anything like that."

"Don't worry about it, sweetheart." Justin tucks me in closer to his side. "Autumn's just looking for an excuse to go shopping."

She nods. "I really am."

"Well then, I guess whatever you want to buy will be wonderful. Thank you."

"My pleasure!" She pulls the door open. "Since Justin's like a brother to me and I can see from how he looks at you that he thinks of you as his, that makes you and the baby mine too."

"Umm, okay," I whisper as the door shuts behind her, not sure what she means.

"She's a bit of a whirlwind, but she means well." Justin tugs me over to the couch, gets me settled on the cushions, and hands me a shopping bag from a department store at the mall. "And she's got great taste in shit like this."

My head is spinning as I pull three blankets out of the bag. The first one is made from a fuzzy cream material, the second is a beige faux fur, and the third is super soft and pink. "They're amazing. Thank you."

"You're welcome." He sits down next to me and kisses the top of my head as I spread the beige blanket over my lap. "We've got to do what we can to keep you relaxed. Stress isn't good for you or the baby."

I cuddle against his muscular chest. "Sorry I was such a mess earlier. These pregnancy hormones are no joke, and I was hoping for better news from the doctor today."

"You don't owe me any apologies, sweetheart. I'm here for whatever you need."

I tilt my head back and search his blue eyes. The only thing I see in them is complete sincerity. "You really mean that, don't you?"

"Of course," he replies softly, and my throat burns.

I know my parents and brothers love me, but I ran away from Vegas because they couldn't see past their anger and be there for me in the way I needed.

It's been a long time since I felt like I had someone who was really on my side. It's really, really nice. So nice that my silly hormones go crazy and I feel my eyes fill with tears. I try to fight them back, but one slips through my lashes then another and another.

"I wasn't trying to make you cry." He swipes his thumbs over my cheeks. "Being here for you is supposed to be a good thing."

I nod and sniffle while I wipe away what's left of my tears.

His blue eyes fill with worry. "Am I fucking up? You need me to back off?"

"No!" That's the last thing I want. After what happened to me the night I got pregnant, I didn't think I'd ever want to get close to a guy, but Justin isn't just anyone. He's kind, funny, and crazy hot. And so patient with me. He's somehow managed to work his way past the wall I'd put up to protect myself before I even realized what he was doing. Now he's inside there with me, close to my heart. Honestly, I didn't stand a chance when it came to falling for him. I grip his wide shoulders, pull him closer, and brush my mouth against his, whispering, "Please don't back off."

"Never," he groans. "That's the only thing you could ask me for that'd be almost impossible to give."

I smile up at him and tilt my head to the side. "What if I want a pony?"

"That'd be doable." His eyes light up and he grins. "The landlord allows pets, but I'm not sure what the rules are when it comes to having a horse. If we couldn't keep one here, we can buy some land."

"I like that idea, but every penny I have is going to the baby right now," I admit as my stomach fills with unease. I hate the idea of him thinking I'm using him for anything. I know he's stable. Even in his twenties, he's living a life most guys would envy. He has a job he loves, where he works from home a lot of the time, and it must pay well, since he has an eighty-two-inch television in his living room and another in his bedroom. He seems to have every game system known to mankind, and uses a computer system unlike anything I've ever seen before with six monitors and a desktop that must be custom-built. Then there's me, living with a roommate, pregnant by another man, and working at a strip club because it's the only job I could get when I moved here.

"Baby." He takes my face in his hands. "I'll get you and the baby anything you need."

"I would never ask you to do that."

"That's the thing—you're not asking me." He kisses my forehead, and a fresh wave of tears fills my eyes.

I never knew men like him existed, men who give without any strings attached. I can only hope that someday I'll be able to stop taking from him and start giving back too.

"Anything you want, it's yours," he says softly.

I open my mouth to say something, anything to express how much he means to me, but instead my stomach chooses that moment to let out a low growl.

He rests his hand on my belly. "Let's start with getting you and my girl some dinner."

His girl. He's killing me.

"I should probably eat something," I agree. "My stomach felt like it was in knots all day, and I don't think I ate enough."

He brushes his lips against mine before getting up and walking over to the kitchen. "Were you that stressed out about going past your due date?" he asks.

"Yeah," I say, rubbing my belly. "The doctor said it's too early to worry, but I still let it get to me. I just want her here already, and carrying her around is taking a toll on my back."

He pulls the leftovers from last night's dinner out of the fridge then looks at me and smiles. "It isn't a pony, but I'll give you a massage after dinner if you want. It might help you relax a little."

"A massage?" I repeat softly, remembering how good it felt to have him rub my feet earlier.

"Yeah, I read online that it's great for stress relief late in pregnancy," he explains, and my cheeks flood with heat and my body tingles at the thought of his strong hands stroking over my naked body. "Would you like that?"

I clear my throat and answer with a quiet "Yeah." Even though I'm not sure how much longer I'll be able to control the hormones raging through my body or the need I have for him.

Chapter 6

Justin

I DON'T THINK I taste a single bite of the food as I shovel it into my mouth. All I can think about is getting my hands on Aubrey's beautiful body. I told her I want to give her a massage to help her relax, but truthfully I want her to get used to my touch.

Even with her only sharing bits and pieces of her past with me, I'm smart enough to know that something dark happened between her and the guy who got her pregnant. There is no other reason a woman like her would want him dead, only she doesn't know that's something I'd be willing to make happen if she ever asked me to. I want her to feel safe. I want her to know I will do whatever I need to do to protect her and her daughter. And since she ran to protect her baby, I know it might come to that. Just as long as when the dust settles we're together I don't give a fuck what goes down.

"That was delicious, thank you." Her soft voice pulls me from my dark thoughts and I focus on her.

"Do you want more?"

"No." She smiles, pushing up off the couch. Once she's standing, I watch her walk by me to take her plate toward the kitchen, and I take my last bite of food then get up and follow her.

"Just leave it," I tell her when she starts to wash her plate. "I'll clean up later."

"I don't mind."

"I know you don't, but I want you relaxed, not doing dishes." I take her plate and set it on top of mine then drop both in the sink. After I shut off the water, I take her hand and lead her toward my bedroom then let her go to walk across the room and flip on the lamp. "Lie down," I say, and she eyes me for a moment before going to the bed.

Seeing her on my bed and smiling at me, my cock twitches. "How do we do this?" she asks.

I know how I'd like to do this. I'd like nothing more than to flip her over so she's up on all fours, slide her pants down her legs, lick her pussy until her juices are dripping down her thighs, then line up my cock and work it into her tightness until I'm settled deep inside her wet heat. I shake my head, clearing the vision of sinking into her, and give an answer that won't scare her off. "We need to get you in a position where I can work on your shoulders and back." I trail my fingers over her rounded stomach before taking a seat on the mattress and leaning back against the headboard. "Come up here and sit down in front of me." I spread my legs to make room for her.

"Okay." Her answer is whisper-soft, but she doesn't hesitate to do as I asked. "Like this?" she asks over her shoulder after she sits with her legs stretched out and her palms pressed against the mattress to help keep her balance.

"That's perfect, sweetheart." I don't miss how her plump lips tilt up at the edges before she turns to face forward again.

My hands are steady as I reach out and begin to softly rub her shoulders. As I stroke my thumbs up her neck, my dick punches against my zipper at how soft her skin is. Every time Aubrey lets me touch her is as good as the first. Better even.

I focus on loosening her muscles with soft, long strokes of my hands. When I feel her shoulders relax, I work my way down her spine to her lower back. She lets out a little mewl as I dig my thumbs into the knots I find there. My fingers still while I try to get myself back under control, because that sound has my cock twitching.

"Don't stop." She sighs. "That feels so good."

I lift the bottom of her shirt and smooth my palms against her warm skin. Then I get back to rubbing the knots out of her muscles. She makes another soft sound, and my head drops forward as I groan. The smell of her fills my nostrils, her coconut and lime shampoo mixed with what I swear is the scent of her desire. I wonder if the massage is turning her on as much as it is me, and it makes me think of something else I read about pregnant women and how helpful orgasms can be.

"I've never had a massage before." She sighs, leaning into my hands. "I had no idea anything could feel this good, but now I can't imagine not getting them on the regular. I don't know how I'll afford it, but I'll have to figure it out so I can get a membership at a spa or something."

What she's saying finally registers in my brain and triggers my inner caveman. "You can have as many massages as you want. All you have to do is ask me for one." I kiss her shoulder. "You feel better?"

"Mmmm," she moans, and my cock throbs. "I don't think I've ever been this relaxed. Thank you."

"You're welcome." I kiss her neck, fighting back the urge to nip her there.

She leans back a little and looks at me over her shoulder. "I think your bed is my new favorite place in the whole world."

I pull her against my chest and wrap my arms around her belly, lacing my fingers with hers. "I'm glad you're feeling better."

"Me too." She gasps suddenly, making my heart race.

"You okay?"

"Yeah… no, I don't know. She's just so big now that every time she moves it takes my breath." She shakes her head. "I wish she'd just come out already."

I rub my hand over her stomach. "There's one more thing I read about that'll relax you even more and might also trigger labor."

"Really? What is it?" She tilts her head back to look up at me.

"There's a hormone that surges when you have an orgasm, and sometimes it triggers labor." I don't mention how there's shit in sperm that can help ripen her cervix. Giving her an orgasm isn't about me getting off, no matter how desperate I am to get inside her.

"An orgasm?" she whispers, her blue eyes wide and full of surprise.

34

"Yeah." I want to say more, but I'm not willing to push her into agreeing. Letting me touch her the way I want to has to be her decision.

I feel her muscles tense back up, and I figure she's going to turn me down. It surprises me when she says, "Umm, so if I just—umm—that's something you'd want to help me with?" Her cheeks are bright red as she stammers, and it only makes me want her more.

"I can definitely help you with that." I slide one hand under the waistband of her leggings, stopping when the tips of my fingers reach the top of her panties.

"You can?"

"Oh yeah." I smooth my fingers over her skin and her muscles bunch. "And I'd love doing it."

Her eyes widen. "You would?"

I dip my fingers into her panties and stroke the soft skin above her pussy. "Fuck yeah."

"Oh." Her eyes close, and she bites her bottom lip. "Umm, I think maybe I—umm—I'd like that."

"I can guarantee you'll more than like it, sweetheart, but I need you to open your eyes while we talk about this." She turns her head and her pretty blue eyes open, I search them for any hint of true fear. I expect her to be at least a little nervous, but I want to make sure her stammering isn't more than that. When I don't find any signs that she's afraid of me touching her, I tell her, "I also need you to tell me it's what you want before I slide my fingers lower, run them through your wetness, and play with your clit until you scream out my name."

Her eyes go wide and fill with desire as her chest rises and falls rapidly. "Please."

It's only one word, but it's more than enough for me. I do exactly what I promised, lightly skimming my fingers over her clit and down to her wetness. Parting her pussy lips, I dip into her tight heat and bury my face against her throat, trailing my tongue over her skin while I work my finger into her. Her legs open wider, bending at the knees to give me more room. My cock is as hard as steel, pressing against her back, but it's worth the blue balls I'll have to feel her tremble in my arms while I send her over the edge.

"You're wet for me, sweetheart, just like I knew you'd be." I glide my finger over her clit again, circling, making her hips buck.

"Justin," she whimpers my name as her fingers dig into my thighs hard enough I can feel her nails through my jeans.

"I'm here with you. I've got you." I slide my free hand up and flick my thumb over her nipple.

"Oh, God," she cries while my finger circles her clit.

I can already feel her body tightening. "You close, sweetheart?"

She gives me a jerky nod. "I... oh, God, please don't stop."

"Never." I sink my finger inside her and flick at her clit with my thumb until she cries out my name. When her pussy stops convulsing, I pull my hand out of her panties and groan, wanting so fucking bad to feel the wetness of her wrapped around my cock. "You okay?"

"Better than okay. I just wish I'd known sooner how amazing orgasms are." She turns to rest her head on my chest so I can't see her face.

"You never had an orgasm?" My gaze goes to the swell of her belly.

"No. Well, I mean I've given them to myself, but they don't begin to compare to how powerful that was." She tucks her fist under her chin while rubbing her cheek against my chest. "I've never even had a real boyfriend. My oldest brother has an... unusual job. It made it hard for me to get close to anyone, because I never knew if they were interested in me for me or if they were trying to get closer to him for one reason or another. He was always cautioning me against getting close to outsiders, and there was no way I would ever date one of his guys, so that left me kind of out in the cold when it came to dating."

I'm curious about what kind of business her brother is in, but that's not what she's trying to tell me about, so it's going to have to wait for another day. "But the father of your baby was different?"

"He was different." She burrows deeper into me and fists her hands in my shirt like she's holding on for dear life. "But not in the way you think. I didn't know who he was. I was out with friends, trying to have some fun, and he was just some guy who didn't seem to understand what the word no meant." My gut twist and my muscles bunch, but she continues. "The girls and I joked about it when he finally backed off, but I should've known it wasn't over. I should've left. I should have gone home where I would've been safe."

I pull in the strength I need to comfort her and not go out and commit murder then stroke my hand down her hair and kiss the top of her head. "Whatever happened, you can't blame yourself. It wasn't your fault."

"That's the worst part, I think. The not knowing," she whispers. "One minute, my friends and I were laughing and ordered another round of drinks. The next, I was waking up in the hospital with no memory of the time in between."

"You don't remember what happened?"

"No, between the drugs he gave me and the blows to the head I'd taken, the doctors said there is only a small chance I'll ever get that time back." Jesus. "He left me for dead, and I tried telling myself that's all it was. I wanted believe I'd pissed him off, so he tried killing me. I wanted to think the doctors were wrong about him raping me." Her shoulders start to shake as she sobs, and my blood heats, making it almost impossible to stay where I am, not when all I want to do is kill the man who hurt her.

"When I turned up pregnant, I couldn't deny it any longer. He took my virginity and left me with an innocent life growing inside me." Her hand covers her belly. "My brother wanted me to get rid of her, but I couldn't do it. It didn't matter to me that my baby could rip apart what he'd built in Vegas. I didn't even care who'd gotten me pregnant. The only thing that mattered to me was protecting *my* baby. Mine, not his. I might not have any memory of what happened to me that night, but I knew my baby was the only good thing that had come out of whatever he did to me."

Vegas. I fucking hate that city and the metric fuck-ton of bad stuff swirling around it. The hit Autumn witnessed before she came to Tennessee, met Kenton, and fell in love, the shit that went down with Kai and Myla, which lead to me pulling the trigger and killing Paulie Jr., and now this. They say what happens in Vegas stays there, but that doesn't seem to be the case. "Do they know where you are?"

"My family?" she asks, tipping her head back to meet my gaze.

"Yeah."

She shakes her head. "No, I didn't tell anyone. I couldn't risk telling

37

my brothers or my parents. I needed to make sure my baby was safe." A fresh wave of tears fills her eyes.

"Shhh." I run my fingers through her hair. "Please don't cry, sweetheart. It's okay. I've got you. I won't let anything happen to you or the baby."

"I know," she whispers, then between one breath and the next, she falls asleep in my arms as though sharing her secret with me gave her the peace she desperately needed.

But my world will never be the same, not until I find vengeance for her.

Chapter 7

Aubrey

*I*T'S DARK WHEN I wake, unsure what pulled me from my sleep. My eyes are still tight and dry from crying earlier, but I feel more rested than I have in a long while. I guess that's what happens when you confess your darkest secret before passing out.

I lift up on my elbow and look down at Justin's gorgeous face through the dark. I can't believe how easy it was to tell him what Paulie Jr. did to me. Nobody in Tennessee knows about my past, not even Shelly. She and Johnny only know I'm pregnant and on my own. Even if they had suspicions, they've never pushed me for details.

Justin didn't push either, but I knew letting him touch me the way he had was a turning point in our relationship, and it was only right to open up about what happened. I'm relieved it's over and I don't need to worry about it anymore. I feel like the ever-present weight in my stomach is gone. He knows the worse of me, and instead of running away, he held me in his arms and proved once more I'm safe in my feelings for him.

I start to lay my head back against his chest but stop when a wave of pain hits me so hard my breath catches. My belly tightens again, and I realize I must be having contractions.

"Justin." I reach out to shake his shoulder, but pain makes me grit my teeth and fall back against the bed, holding my stomach. "Oh, God."

"Aubrey?" Justin shoots up and looms over me, placing his hand over mine. "What's wrong?"

"I... I..." I pant, squeezing my eyes closed. "I think I'm going into labor."

"What?" He shakes his head like he's still trying to wake up.

I lean up, letting out a sigh of relief as the contraction ends. "I'm in labor."

"You're having the baby?" His gaze drops to my belly right before he hops out of bed, wearing only a T-shirt and pair of boxer briefs. I've never seen him without any pants on, and his butt looks even better wrapped in just a thin layer of stretchy material. My view of it doesn't last for long, because he yanks on a pair of sweats and sits down on the edge of the mattress to put on his shoes. When he gets up, he grabs his wallet and cell from the bedside table and shoves both into his pocket. "Your shoes and purse are in the living room. I'll grab 'em for you. You need to grab anything else before we head to the hospital?" He turns to find me in the bed still dressed in my leggings and shirt with bare feet.

"I have a bag packed for the hospital." I start to scoot toward the edge of the bed but stop when he reaches out and helps me up.

"Is it in Shelly's apartment?"

I nod, liking that he calls it her place and not mine. I feel more comfortable with him here than I ever did living with Shelly. "Yeah, it's in my room, just inside as soon as you step through the door."

"All right." He kisses my forehead swiftly then leads me into the living room and gets me settled on the couch before bringing my shoes over. He drops down to his knees in front of me and slides them on my feet. When they're on, he leans forward and brushes his lips against mine. "Stay right here. I'm going to run and grab your stuff. Then I'll take you to the hospital."

I shake my head. "I think it's too early."

"Hospital's open twenty-four seven, sweetheart. There's no such thing as too early."

I point to my belly and smile. "No, I mean it's too early in my labor. I've only had one contraction. I'm not even sure how far apart they are, because I haven't had another one since the first one hit. The doctor said it usually takes longer with your first baby. I'm not supposed to go to the hospital until they're like five minutes apart or my water breaks, and I think I have to call the office first to make sure it isn't just Braxton Hicks that are false labor pains that don't help things along, no matter how painful they might be," I mutter, praying that's not what I'm feeling right now. It would really suck to go through that pain again if I'm not really in labor.

He shakes his head as he walks to the door. "The shit you women have to go through for the miracle of birth."

"You can say that again." I blow a piece of hair out of my face and he smiles.

"Here's the plan." He opens the door. "I'll grab your bag so we're ready, and then we'll keep track of your contractions. If they even come close to being five minutes apart, we'll head to the hospital. Which one is your doctor at?"

"Vanderbilt."

"Perfect. If it's a problem, I'll call Autumn and see if she can pull any strings for us, since she's a nurse there."

I don't think hospitals work that way, but he seems so confident that I don't want to burst his bubble. Plus, I have no doubt that he'll figure out how to get me admitted if it comes down to that. Honestly, it's reassuring, especially since I figured I'd be alone when the time came to give birth to my baby girl. This is so much better than my recurring nightmare where I had to drive myself to the hospital but couldn't get the door to my car open and I ended up giving birth in the parking lot instead.

While he's gone, I get up and go to the bathroom, wash my hands, splash some water on my face, and brush my teeth with an extra toothbrush I find in one of the drawers. When I pad back out to the living room, I feel a little more refreshed, but I am in no way ready for the next contraction as it hits me. This one is stronger than the other one I felt, and it almost drops me to my knees. I rest against the wall and attempt to breathe through the pain.

"Why are you up?" Justin asks, dropping my bag off his shoulder and rushing to my side as soon as he comes through the door. "Did you have another one?"

"Yes." I lean into him and let him help me back to the couch. I take a deep breath through my nose and let it out through my mouth. "It's over now." I sigh in relief and lean back against the cushion.

"I don't think I was gone for even five minutes." The worry in his tone is audible.

"I don't think you were either."

"C'mon." He tugs on my hand and leads me to the door. "I can't handle seeing you in that much pain. We're going to the hospital."

"But—"

He doesn't let me finish. He goes and grabs my bag then comes back to the couch and picks me up. Cradled in the safety of his embrace, I wrap my arms around his shoulders as he carries me out the door. "You can call your doctor on the way. At the rate you're having contractions, you'll have four more before I even get you to the hospital."

"Okay." I'm not about to argue with him, not when I'm seriously scared myself by how quickly each one seems to be coming. Especially when I read it's normal to be in pre-labor for hours with your first baby.

"Let me help." He takes the seatbelt from my shaking hands once he has me in the passenger seat of his Rover.

"Thank you," I whisper, and his eyes linger over my face before he clicks my buckle into place.

"Anything," he whispers back, brushing his lips over mine before moving out the door and slamming it closed. A moment later, he climbs behind the wheel then reaches over and laces his fingers through mine, giving them a squeeze. "I know it's got to be hard as fuck for you to trust me, baby, but I promise you'll never regret it." He starts the engine and pulls out of the parking lot.

"It's actually easy trusting you," I admit quietly as he drives. Yes, my brain might've needed a little more time to catch up, but my heart seemed to know right away that he was the kind of guy any woman would be lucky to have, including me.

"That's good to know," he says, and I start to laugh, but it's cut off by another contraction. While I breathe through it, his gaze darts to the clock on the dash as he steps on the gas to speed up.

42

A little less than a minute later, the pain passes, and I pant, "You're everything I didn't expect to find."

"Fuck, sweetheart," he groans. "How can you be so damn sweet when you're in labor? Aren't you supposed to be yelling and screaming at me?"

"Do you want me to yell at you?"

"Not really," he says, squeezing my fingers, and I laugh as he stops at a red light and turns to look at me. "Seriously, baby. If anyone in this car is lucky, it's me, not you."

"I think that goes to prove I'm right about you." I shift in my seat, trying to get comfortable now that my lower back is aching. It doesn't do any good, and I grimace at the pain.

"What's wrong?" he asks, his tone full of worry.

I try to smile at him, but my attempt doesn't appear to reassure him much. "The contraction's over, but now my back hurts." Tears fill my eyes as I start to freak out. "What if the recurring nightmare I've had about giving birth in the parking lot all by myself was a warning? What if we should've called an ambulance? What if—"

"Aubrey," he bites out in a firm, deep voice, cutting me off. "Take a deep breath, baby."

I squeeze my eyes shut and focus on my breathing. "Okay, you're right. I need to try to stay calm. Even if you have to pull over before we make it to the hospital, it's not like I'll be alone."

"I'm not going to have to pull over so you can give birth. Your doctor said the first time you give birth takes the longest, remember?" he reassures me. I give him a jerky nod and keep on breathing. "We're halfway there already. You're doing great."

"So are you," I say, and he laughs, thinking I'm joking when I'm not. I'm almost sure most men wouldn't be this calm and understanding in the same situation.

"All I'm doing is driving, sweetheart. You're the one who's doing all the hard work."

"You're not just driving." My throat gets tight. "You're here for me."

"Damn straight I'm here, and I'll *never* let you be alone again if you let me."

I turn my head, open my eyes, and stare at him in silence as he drives for another minute or so before all the muscles in my lower abdominal area squeeze tight and I have to pant through the pain again. When it passes, I whisper, "You better be careful what you offer right now, because I might hold you to it, Justin."

"Go ahead, Aubrey. Don't you get it? I want you to hold me to it for the rest of our lives."

Chapter 8

Justin

When WE PULL up in front of the hospital, I throw the Rover into Park and haul ass around to the passenger side as a guy wearing a uniform steps out through the sliding doors. "What's going on?"

"My girl's in labor," I tell him, and he grabs a wheelchair while I grab her bag from the backseat.

"You can't leave your car here, man," he says as I slam the door shut and turn to follow him.

"There's no way I'm letting my girl out of my sight when the baby could be here any minute." He opens his mouth, and I know he's about to tell me that the Rover will get towed if I leave it there. I couldn't give a fuck, since Aubrey is what's important to me at the moment. But I figure there's an easy solution so I don't need to track my vehicle down when she and the baby are discharged. "There's a hundred bucks in it for you if you'll park it and bring me the keys and parking garage ticket when you're done."

Aubrey looks over her shoulder, rolling her eyes at me. "We just got here and you're already bribing hospital employees?"

"It's not a bribe. It's asking someone to do a favor in return for money."

"Yeah, it's a favor." The attendant holds out his hand for my key then steps away from the wheelchair, letting me push it as he walks toward the Rover. "And if you decide you need any more favors while you're here, I'm your man."

"How much money do you have left in your wallet?" Aubrey asks ten minutes and five contractions later while we're still waiting to go back to a room.

"Probably a couple hundred bucks, but I'm sure there's an ATM around here somewhere." I look up at her from the paperwork they handed us when we got here. "Why? You need something?"

"Yeah," she pants. "A bribe for the nurse to get me into a room now!"

I press a kiss to her forehead then rise from my chair. "Gimme a second and I'll take care of it."

She gives me a jerky nod, and I stalk over to the desk. "How much longer? My woman is about ready to deliver her baby right here in your waiting room."

"It'll be just a few more minutes," the woman dressed in scrubs says without even bothering to look up from her cell phone.

I lean closer and slam down the clipboard. "Put your goddamn phone down and do your fucking job."

That finally gets her attention, and her head jerks up. "Step back and do not swear at me again. If you do, I'll call security and have you kicked out." Her lip curls up in disdain as she mutters, "Medicaid patients are the worst. Popping out babies left and right, expecting the rest of us to cover their bills while they demand the best of everything."

Her tone is low, but I still caught what she said. "Pardon?" I fight the urge to jump over the counter and strangle her scrawny ass.

"Sir." Another nurse moves next to me and wraps her hand around my bicep, pulling my attention off the woman I'm currently glaring at. "I have Aubrey's room ready for her."

"It'd better be a private room after the shit that nurse just spewed," I grumble. "If it comes down to it, I'll pay the difference."

"No worries there. All we have are private rooms in this unit." She beams a smile at me as she moves over to Aubrey's wheelchair and starts to wheel it toward the hallway leading to the rooms. "And even if we didn't, I'd make sure your girl got one anyway, after you guys had to put up with Marni's drama. You shouldn't have had to wait that long or hear her say crap like that."

"What happened?" Aubrey asks.

I reach down and squeeze her hand. "The girl at the desk was in no rush to get you admitted, because she was too busy being a bitch about your insurance."

"It isn't the first time someone's had something bad to say about me being pregnant with a 'Medicaid baby.'" She shrugs her shoulders. "But it's not like I have a lot of options. Johnny doesn't offer health insurance, and I can't ask my family for help. Not after what they asked me to do."

I make a mental note to ask Kenton what it would take to get Aubrey and the baby added to my policy. We're covered for just about anything with almost no deductible, which is a smart move on his part considering some of the risks we take for the job.

"Marni's behavior today was unacceptable and is the last bit of evidence I need for Human Resources so they can finally fire her. Please trust me when I tell you that you won't be hearing anything like that from anyone else."

"Let me know if you need me to file a complaint," I offer as I help Aubrey out of the wheelchair and onto the bed.

"It would be helpful," she says as Aubrey has another contraction. Once it passes, we help her change into a hospital gown and lie back against the pillow.

"I'm so thirsty." Aubrey's face contorts in pain with another contraction and I eye the clock. I haven't been keeping track, but they seem to be coming even closer together.

"Can you get her some water?" I ask the nurse.

She shakes her head while picking up the pink plastic pitcher on the table next to the bed. "She can't have water, but you can feed her some ice chips. They'll help with the dry mouth."

Aubrey lets out a little whimper, and I press a kiss against her sweaty forehead. "Sorry, baby. I promise once the baby's here and you've got the all-clear from your doctor, I'll get you whatever you want to drink."

"Even a milkshake from Lulu's?"

Lulu's is an old-fashioned diner about an hour north of us, but that doesn't change my answer. "If a milkshake from Lulu's is what you want, then that's exactly what you'll get. As often as you want them."

"Awww, I wish all the daddies were as sweet as you," the nurse says, handing off the pitcher of ice chips and a spoon to me.

"He's not the father," Aubrey admits softly with tears in her eyes. I have to swallow down a lump in my throat, and it's not just because I know she's remembering how she got pregnant. It's also because there's a big part of me that wants to lay claim to her daughter and her.

Aubrey squeezes my hand, and I focus on her beautiful face. "You're the only person in the world I want to have with me when she comes into this world."

"Just try and get rid of me."

The nurse laughs. "I'm not volunteering for that job. I can only imagine how many security guards it would take to rip you from her side."

"All of them," I mutter, knowing damn well I'd fight to my last breath to stay at her side now that she's let me in.

Aubrey's hold on my hand tightens to the point of pain, and I breathe a sigh of relief when the doctor finally arrives. Things move quickly from there, and a sense of pride fills me with how well Aubrey holds up through it all.

"Sorry, it's too late for an epidural," the doctor says, lowering the sheet back into place after checking her.

"She's in pain," I point out.

He looks at me. "I know, but unfortunately she's progressing too fast for her to get one now." He pats my arm after he stands and says, "She'll be okay."

I want to punch him in the face and ask if he'll be okay, but I don't. Instead, I focus on Aubrey for the next hour and a half, whispering words of encouragement and feeding her ice chips. When the time comes, I hold one of her legs back until the beautiful sound of a baby crying fills the room.

"It's a girl!" the doctor confirms.

I look up and lock eyes on Aubrey's daughter for the first time, feeling my heart pounds hard in my chest. One look and I'm done for.

She already owns my soul, just like her mom does.

I divide my attention between both my girls as the doctor finishes up with Aubrey and the nurses check over the baby before cleaning her up. When all the excitement is over, the nurse places the baby in Aubrey's arms.

"She's beautiful," she whispers, tracing a shaking finger over the baby's cheek.

"Just like her mommy," I agree.

"Have you picked out a name yet?" the nurse asks.

"No."

"Yes."

Aubrey and I answer at the same time, and I'm surprised, because the last time we talked, she told me she hadn't decided for sure yet. "What did you decide on, baby?"

"I'd like to name her Jenna Ann."

"A beautiful name for a beautiful girl." The nurse writes the baby's name down onto a notecard and places it in the bassinet in the corner of the room.

Aubrey smiles at me, but there's a hint of worry in her tired blue eyes. Wanting to wipe that look away, I brush a kiss against the top of her head and whisper, "You did good. Jenna Ann is the perfect name for her."

"It's more perfect than you know." She looks down at Jenna's sweet sleeping face and touches her cheek. "There's a tradition in my family when it comes to naming babies," she admits softly as she takes my hand and holds on tight.

She doesn't talk about her family much, which I get, considering everything she's been through. I figure that bringing them up now is a big deal for her, and I hook my foot around the chair leg at the end of the bed and pull it toward me so I can drop down into it without letting go of her hand. "Did the tradition help you pick Jenna's name?"

"Yeah." She shifts her gaze to me and her cheeks fill with a pretty pink color. "But you helped more."

Even tired from giving birth to Jenna, with her hair a tangle of curls and dark circles under her eyes, she's so fucking beautiful that I have to

49

lean over and brush a kiss over her lips before I ask, "How'd I help?"

"The baby's middle name always has the same initial as their mom, so Ann is for Aubrey, since I'm her mama."

It's like the whole world stops for a moment when it hits me what she's about to say next. The nurse is still in the room with us, but the only people who matter to me right now are Aubrey and Jenna. I want this to be just ours for now, so I get up and bend over the bed, caging Aubrey in by pressing my hands into the mattress on either side of her head. Then I drop my forehead against hers and ask in the barest of whispers, "And her first name?"

"It's supposed to be the same initial as her father, but I couldn't do it. He doesn't get to touch any part of my precious girl, not her name. Nothing."

"Of course he doesn't, sweetheart. He'd have to go through me to get to either of you, and that's never gonna happen," I swear.

Her eyes fill with tears and she nods. "When the nurse asked about her name, you popped into my head, the way you've taken care of me, the way you looked at her. It felt... right. I know I probably should've asked first, but... I—"

"Don't ever try to apologize to me for this again." I cup her cheeks with my palms and swipe the tears on her cheeks away with my thumbs. "Naming her Jenna after me? I'm so fucking honored and proud." I have to swallow down a lump in my throat before I can continue. "I promise I'll do right by both of you and earn that gift you just gave me."

"Justin," she whispers.

"Promise, Aubrey." I squeeze her hand and touch my fingers to Jenna's cheek, knowing that she and her mommy were always meant to be mine.

Chapter 9

Aubrey

I SMILE AT the nurse when she quietly enters the room then watch her get a soft look on her face when she searches for Jenna and finds her cuddled in Justin's arms, both of them asleep in a chair next to my bed.

"You doing okay, honey?" She comes toward me, pulling the cart with a blood pressure cuff and thermometer attached.

"Yeah." I look over at the man in the chair next to my bed, holding my beautiful girl, thinking good doesn't even express half of what I am right now as she takes my vitals.

"Are you in the mood for company?"

"Company?"

She turns to look at me as she writes down the information from the machine on the whiteboard on the wall at the end of my bed. "There's a whole bunch of people out in the waiting room who are looking forward to meeting your little beauty."

"Are you sure they aren't here for someone else?"

"I'm sure." She smiles then says, "If you're okay with them coming in, just press your call button and let the desk know."

"Okay," I reply, wondering who could be here.

"Do you need anything else right now?"

"I think I'm okay for now." I watch her nod, and when she leaves,

I look at Justin and see his eyes are open and on me. "The nurse said people are here."

"I heard. Do you feel up to having people around?"

"I don't know," I admit quietly. There's a very short list of people I'd be comfortable having in the room with Jenna so soon. She was only born a few hours ago, but that doesn't mean that my maternal instincts aren't already in full swing. "Would you mind going out there to see who it is?"

"I don't even need to leave the room to figure that out." He offers me a reassuring smile as he shifts his hold on Jenna so he can pull his phone out of his pocket. "Kenton sent me a text when the lactation consultant was here to help you get Jenna to latch on the first time. He and Autumn were getting ready to come to the hospital to check on us. They should be here by now. I can ask him who else is out there with them."

"Your friends came to check on us?" My voice wavers at the end, and Justin's head jerks up. After he scans my face, he drops his phone in his lap and reaches out to take my hand. I give him a weak smile and explain, "It's just been awhile since I've had people in my life who care enough to go out of their way. I… I thought I left that behind in Vegas with my family."

"Baby," he whispers, and my gaze drops to Jenna as my eyes fill with tears. It hurts to think she might never get the chance to know her grandparents or uncles.

"Hey, now." He rises from the chair, with my sweet little girl nestled in his strong arms. Once he settles on the edge of my bed, he places his hand on my cheek. "You're not alone anymore. You've got me, and I'm not going anywhere."

I wipe the tears off my cheeks and reach for my baby girl, needing to hold her. Once I have her cuddled against my chest, he places his forehead against mine then drops a kiss to my lips and pulls away. I tilt my head back and smile at him. "I never thought I'd say this, but I'm actually grateful for my piece-of-crap car."

His brow wrinkles in confusion. "What?"

"If it wasn't for that hunk of junk, who knows if we would have ever gotten together."

His blue eyes lock on mine as he shakes his head. "Your fucked up car might've given me a push to make my move, but I noticed you long before that."

What he just said registers, and I tip my head to the side. "You noticed me before you gave me a ride to work the first time?"

"Babe." He strokes Jenna's palm with a finger, and her tiny hand clamps around it. "You're hard to miss."

I look down at my belly, which I thought would've gone down more now that I gave birth. "Yeah, I guess I was."

"It wasn't your belly that caught my attention." He loops a lock of my hair around one of his fingers. "I didn't even notice you were pregnant until after I saw your long blonde hair and perfect ass."

"Really?" I narrow my eyes on him.

"What can I say? I'm a man." He brushes his lips against my cheek before shrugging his broad shoulders. "Still, it wasn't your looks that kept my attention. It was your sweet disposition and courage."

"Courage?" My nose wrinkles. "I hate to be the one to break it to you, but I'm the least courageous person I know."

"Only because you don't see yourself the way I do." He glances at his phone when it beeps. "And I must not be the only one."

"What?"

"Kenton says there's a whole group in the waiting room. Shelly, Johnny, and a few girls from Dolly's."

My eyes go wide in surprise. "Really?"

"Yeah." He pulls his eyes off his phone to look at me. "How do you feel about having a few visitors?"

"I don't know." I look down at Jenna, who is nestled in the crook of my arm, and then lift my other hand to tuck my hair behind my ears. "She's just so new, and I'm sure I look like crap."

He bends his head, sliding his nose against mine, whispering against my lips, "It's your call, sweetheart, but you should know you look more beautiful than I've ever seen you."

I sigh. "I guess it wouldn't hurt to have company, but can I have my bag, so I can brush my hair?"

He brings it to me then lifts Jenna off my chest. "Do whatever shit you *think* you need to do to make yourself prettier than you already are, even though you don't need to."

"You're good for my ego." I give him a tired smile when he chuckles then dig through my bag for my brush and makeup kit. I tie my hair up into a ponytail and swipe on some mascara then give up, too tired to do more. I drop my bag on the floor by my bed and settle back against the pillow, in as much of a sitting position as the hospital bed will allow. "Maybe if I'm holding her, no one will notice me," I say, reaching out my hands for Jenna.

He shakes his head and laughs before crossing the floor to give Jenna to me. After I get her settled in my arms, he tilts my head back with a finger under my chin and brushes his lips across mine. "You're fucking gorgeous."

"Thank you." I rub my hand against the five o'clock shadow on his cheek, enjoying the feel of it against my skin. "You're not too shabby yourself, especially when you're all scruffy like this. But you're going to have to clean up your language around the baby. I don't think it would be a good thing if her first word was an F-bomb."

"Our girl's not even a day old yet." He grins. "I think I have time to work on how often I swear before it's going to be a problem.

Our girl. I love that, and I really love how he talks about the future like he fully expects to be in Jenna's life and mine. Honestly, I'm not sure what I would've done without him today or the past few weeks. Meeting him changed everything, and for the first time in a long time, I don't feel alone.

Looking down at my precious baby girl, it hits me how much I miss my family and just how much they're going to miss out on. They won't hear Jenna's first words or see her first steps. They won't be around to watch her unwrap presents for the holidays. My brother Aedan, who taught me how to ride a bike, won't get the chance to do the same with her, and all because he and the rest of my family refused to listen to me when I told them I wanted to keep her. I know Aedan worked hard to build his empire, but I'm hurt his business was more important than my happiness and my beautiful girl.

"Hey," Justin whispers, wiping the tears I didn't even notice from my cheeks with his thumbs. "What's wrong, baby?"

"Just thinking about my family." I breathe deep, trying to get ahold of my runaway emotions. "I wish things were different so they could be in her life." I stroke a finger down her soft cheek, still amazed I created her.

"I bet if they met her, they'd see how special she is and understand why you fought to keep her."

I wish the situation was that simple, but between Aedan's position in the Las Vegas criminal world and his connection to Jenna's sperm donor, it's much more complicated.

"Maybe," I agree, not wanting to get into the reasons that will never happen.

"No more tears, okay? No matter what, I'll be by your side," he assures, and I try to smile, but instead more tears fall, and his expression fills with worry. "You sure you're up for visitors?"

I swipe away the last few tears on my cheeks and nod. "Yeah, go ahead and let them know they can come in. I hate that they've been waiting."

"Fuck all of them," he rasps, cupping the back of Jenna's tiny head and my cheek in each of his large hands. "You two are what's important." The gesture and his words are so sweet I almost start to cry again. Instead, I pull in a few deep breaths.

"I think I'm okay now."

"You sure?" *No*, I want to say, but I don't. Instead, I give him a nod. He studies me for a moment then sends a text to his friend. A few minutes later, my hospital room is full of visitors. Kenton and Autumn bring in a huge teddy bear and a bouquet of pink mylar balloons. Johnny has a bag full of takeout from my favorite deli. Shelly, Maria, Lana, and Stella have a new outfit for Jenna with a matching cap and booties and a few other odds and ends I know I will need.

"You guys didn't need to bring anything." I hand the outfit to Justin as he gives me the sandwich he unwrapped. I'm hesitant to eat it in front of everyone, because it feels rude, but it's hard since I'm starving.

"Eat up, girl. I know you've got to be hungry," Johnny says softly, touching my hair, and I smile up at him before taking a bite of roast beef and melted cheese on soft, doughy bread.

"I know every time I gave birth I felt like I just finished a triathlon," Stella says, and Maria nods in agreement.

"When have you ever ran in your life?" Shelly asks, rolling her eyes.

"I chase after my kids every day. They don't have an off switch; they just keep going and going and going." Stella shrugs.

"The upside is they keep you in shape." Lana smiles.

"I guess that's something to look forward to when Jenna gets big enough to run wild around our apartment," Shelly says, not appearing like she's looking forward to that at all, which makes me wonder how long she's going to be okay with us living with her. Worry fills my stomach. I'm not sure how I'm going to afford a place of my own, but I might have to figure it out sooner rather than later.

Justin's eyes lock on mine, and he must misinterpret my expression, because he turns to Autumn who's holding Jenna. "Sorry, Sweetcheeks. Visiting time is over."

"Aww, but I'm not ready to give up baby cuddles yet," she complains as she transfers Jenna over to him.

"Then you need to get your own," he mutters, kissing the top of my girl's head and making Autumn laugh. But I notice Kenton looking at her with an intensity in his eyes that tells me it won't be long before they have a little one of their own if he has his way.

"He definitely has my approval. You landed yourself a good one, girl," Stella whispers in my ear, giving me a hug, which is followed by quick hugs from the rest of the girls and Johnny. Each of them give Justin much the same approval before they leave. Their admiration doesn't really surprise me, since Justin is the best man I've ever known. I just hope I can be what he needs and that my daughter and I won't be too much for him to handle.

Chapter 10

Justin

"I'LL BE BACK in a few minutes," I tell Aubrey while I gently place Jenna in the bassinet next to her bed.

"Sure." She gives me a tired smile, and I lean over to kiss her then touch Jenna's head and order, "Try to sleep."

She nods, and I kiss the top of her head then follow Kenton and Autumn out of the room.

"Babe, you mind giving me and Justin a minute?" Kenton asks Autumn when the door closes.

She glances between the two of us and sighs. "You've got something you need to talk to Justin about that you don't want me to hear?"

"Babe." He shakes his head, knowing she's never been the kind of woman to not ask questions.

"Fine, I'll go down and check out the gift shop." She holds out her hand and wiggles her fingers. He grins, pulling out his wallet and giving her a twenty, and she takes it then tugs out a hundred-dollar bill, winking at me. "I'll find something for Jenna."

"Hold up," he orders as she turns to walk away, and she twirls back around.

"What?"

"You're forgetting something."

I shake my head as he takes her hand and pulls her close. A lot of other guys would give her a hard time for digging into their wallet, but I know he's more concerned with letting her leave without a kiss.

A light blush creeps across her cheeks as she rises up on her toes, and he slides his hand into her hair to claim her mouth, not bothered at all by the employees at the nurses' station who stop and stare at them. When he ends the kiss, she blinks a few times before giving me a crooked smile and turning to head down the hallway.

We watch her until she rounds the corner, out of sight, and then he nudges my shoulder, gaining my attention. "Looks like you've fallen hard." He jerks his chin toward Aubrey's room.

I scrub my hands down my face, the tired gesture hiding my smile. I never thought I'd fall this hard or this fast for someone before Aubrey came into my life. "Yeah." I shake my head.

He pats my back. "I'm happy as fuck for you, man."

"Thanks."

"She's sweet, but she doesn't seem the type to work in a strip club."

I narrow my eyes, ready to blast him if any negative shit comes out of his mouth, knowing he royally fucked up when he first met Autumn, because he judged her for being a stripper.

He takes a step back and holds his hands up with his palms facing me. "You know I don't mean it like that. All I'm trying to say is that I feel like there's a story behind how she ended up there, and I can't help but wonder if it's why I'm only now just meeting her. You need my help? Because you've got to know I'm here for you and her, no matter what it is."

I run my fingers through my hair, not allowing my feelings to show on my face. "What happened to Aubrey is hers to share. It's not my place to tell you that shit."

"Is it bad?"

I squeeze my eyes shut, refusing to think about what she went through, especially so soon after the miracle of Jenna's birth. The bastard who hurt her doesn't deserve any part in today. "All I'm going to say right now is if I need your help, I'll let you know."

He quirks a brow at me and crosses his arms over his chest. "You're the nosiest fucker I know, and you have access to a world of information at your fingertips. Are you really going to stand there and tell me you haven't run a background check on her?"

I cross my arms over my chest, copying his stance, and a muscle in his jaw twitches.

"Don't make the same mistakes I did," he adds.

I give him a jerk of my chin to let him know I hear him but don't say anything.

Before Aubrey opened up to me last night, I resisted the urge to dig into her past. But now that I know about her being raped and beaten, all bets are off. The only reason I haven't looked into things is because I haven't had time. Last night, I couldn't bear to leave her in bed by herself after everything she shared with me. And I didn't want to run the risk of her waking up alone and thinking it was because I looked at her differently now that I know her story.

I never want her to wonder about that, not even for a second. So I fell asleep with her in my arms and woke up this morning to her needing to be rushed to the hospital. Now that Jenna's here, digging into her past is on the top of my list of shit I need to do—second only to making sure she has everything she needs while she's in the hospital.

I twine my fingers with Aubrey's and smile. "Relax, sweetheart. I stopped by the fire station and had them check the car seat base to make sure it's installed the right way, and while I was there, they showed me how to strap her in. I won't let anything happen to her," I say, and she twists back around to face forward in her seat. For the last two days, I've barely left her and Jenna's sides except to run home a few times to make sure everything was being set up correctly.

"I'm just so nervous. Is it normal to be this nervous?"

"I think so." I glance at the speedometer to make sure I'm not going over the limit, something I usually don't pay much attention to.

She squeezes my hand. "Thank you."

"For what?"

"Everything. We're so lucky to have you in our lives. I don't know what I would have done without you. It's going to be weird not waking up and seeing you next to my bed," she says, giving me the perfect opening.

"There's something I want to talk to you about." I stop at a red light and turn to look at her. "I was hoping you and Jenna would move in with me instead of staying with Shelly. My place is quieter than hers, and it'll make it easier for me to help. Plus, you shouldn't be on your own so soon after having a baby."

She tilts her head to the side, causing a lock of blonde hair to slide over her shoulder. "Those all sound like good reasons for me to want to move in with you, but it doesn't explain why you'd want that. Having Jenna at your place will probably mess up your schedule. She's going to be up all hours of the night and crying during the day. You probably won't be able to get much sleep or concentrate on work."

"You're leaving out the fact that I'll have you both with me, which is what I want."

She leans back against the headrest and sighs. "How is it you always know the perfect thing to say?"

"Because I'm perfect." I wink, and her lips tilt up in a smile, while her blue eyes light up.

I pull into the parking lot in front of our apartment building and snag the spot right in front of the doors, cutting off the engine. I turn to face her, wanting her to see how serious I am about this. "The only thing I want to hear you say right now is that you'll move in with me."

She looks back at Jenna. "I'm tempted to say yes, because I'm already worried about how things will go with Shelly. She gave me a place to stay, and I'll always owe her for that, but I'm not sure how she'll feel when I have to ask her and her friends to keep it down because the baby is sleeping." She looks at me and nibbles her bottom lip. "I just don't want us to be an inconvenience to you."

"Neither of you could ever be an inconvenience." I take her hand in mine. "Do you trust me?"

"Yes." She surprises me by answering immediately.

"Then come inside with me." I lift her hand to my lips and kiss her fingertips.

"Okay," she agrees.

I climb out and round the hood to help her out of the passenger side then grab her bag. I swing it over my shoulder before removing Jenna's carrier from the base. I close the door with my hip and follow Aubrey into the building. When she stops at my door, I yank my keys out of my pocket to unlock it and wave her inside. Heading down the hall straight for the bedroom, where most of the stuff is set up, I nudge the door open.

"Oh my God." She gasps, seeing the bassinet from her room at Shelly's inside, along with the stuff I asked my mom to pick up for her and Jenna. "So Shelly knew about this?"

"She did." Honestly, she didn't seem surprised when I asked her to help me bring all the baby stuff to my place. Something I was glad I did before they were discharged from the hospital, since she only had the bare necessities. A long phone call to my mom, in which I explained about Aubrey and Jenna, fixed that.

"This is beautiful." She runs her hand over the soft pink blanket hanging over the side of the bassinet.

"My mom picked that," I tell her as she picks it up, rubbing it against her cheek.

"Your mom?" Her eyes widen slightly. "You told your mom about me?"

"Baby, I plan on you and Jenna being a part of my life. Of course I told my mom about you. She was mad I hadn't mentioned you sooner, but she's excited to meet you and Jenna, and is planning on coming to visit when you're ready for company."

"I… I'd love to meet her."

"I want you to be happy here." I drop the bag on the end of my bed and set the baby carrier in the middle of the mattress. Then I go to Aubrey and cup her cheeks with my palms, brushing my lips against hers. "I tried to make sure you have everything else you need. There's a stroller in the back of the Rover that goes with her car seat, a changing table and diaper disposal thing in the bathroom, a state-of-the-art monitoring system we can use when she's sleeping, and a fuck-ton of outfits for her stacked on the shelves in my closet. Oh, and a whole mess of stuff in the kitchen in case you decide to bottle feed her."

"I… I… I don't even know what to say," she stammers.

"Say that you'll stay."

"Okay," she whispers with tears filling her eyes. "But promise you'll tell me if we become too much."

I ignore her statement and lead her over to the bed. "Why don't you lie down for a little bit while Jenna's sleeping? And I'll make something for us to eat later."

"You're going to cook?"

I turn to look at her as I unhook Jenna from her car seat. "Okay, I'll order us something later," I amend, catching her smile as I place Jenna in her bassinet while Aubrey gets comfortable in my bed.

"Thank you."

"Anything." I walk to where she's laying and kiss the top of her head. Before I even leave the room, she's fast asleep, so I grab the screen for the monitor and bring it into the living room, leaving the door open a crack behind me. I'm not sure how long they'll sleep, but my guess is it won't be long before Jenna will need to eat again.

I hurry over to my laptop and fire it up then take it with me to the couch. The last couple days have been too busy for me to worry about anything but Aubrey and the baby. But now that I have them home with me where they belong, I start my search for the man I plan on killing.

Chapter 11

Aubrey

"*I* HAVE BAD news," Justin says, coming into the bedroom, and my heart drops into my stomach.

"Bad news?" I repeat, studying him as he takes Jenna who is asleep in my arms and moves her to the bassinet.

"It's going to be okay."

"Okay." I wait for him to say more, but he doesn't. "Are you going to tell me what the bad news that's going to be okay is?"

"My parents will be here in half an hour."

My head jerks back and I stare at him in shock. I really hope my foggy brain imagined what he just said. Even with all of the help he's giving me, I feel exhausted. Jenna barely cries, but she only catnaps on and off between feedings every hour and a half, so I'm not getting much sleep. "I'm sorry, but did you just say your parents are coming over?"

"Yeah, I couldn't put my mom off any longer. She's been calling me at least twice a day, asking if we're ready for visitors yet. This morning, I guess she decided to skip the call, because my dad just sent me a text to let me know they're on their way."

I get up, taking the baby monitor with me, and leave the room, knowing he'll follow. I hear him shut the door softly behind us and go to the kitchen, setting the monitor on the counter before I turn to face him.

"I'm not ready for visitors."

"Stella stopped by yesterday afternoon," he points out, grabbing my hand and leading me to the couch, taking a seat before pulling me down onto his lap.

"Yeah, but that was just Stella. I don't need to impress her, because she already knows me. She doesn't care what I look like. Your parents are a different story." I blow out a breath. "The last time I remember brushing my hair was a few days ago when I was still in the hospital. I've taken a couple quick showers, but I haven't had time to shave my legs. I'm in no way prepared to meet your parents."

"Baby, relax. I'm sure my mom and dad remember what it's like to have a newborn. They're not going to judge you for being a new mom." I snort, and he tugs me closer and rests his chin on my shoulder. "Trust me. You couldn't look bad if you tried."

I melt against him. "There's no way I'd feel comfortable meeting your parents without at least taking a shower, washing my hair, and changing into my own clothes. So if they're really on their way over here, I better get moving."

He loosens his hold on me, and I slide off his lap.

"Go on," he urges. "I've got Jenna covered if she wakes up."

I pause in the doorway when I see the time out the corner of my eye. "It's almost time for lunch. Do we have anything besides sandwiches that we can make for your parents?"

He waves off my concern. "Don't worry about it. I'm sure my mom will have it covered. No matter how many times I tell her not to, she stocks my fridge whenever she comes over, and I highly doubt today will be any different. If anything, she'll probably go even more overboard than usual, because she'll be nervous about meeting you and excited about finally getting to hold Jenna."

It's hard for me to believe she might be as nervous as me, but for all I know, it's normal. I've never had a boyfriend before, so I haven't experienced the whole meeting the parents thing. "You really think so?"

He nods. "After a week of waiting, she's probably a mess of nerves by now."

"A week, huh?" I shake my head. "It feels like it was just yesterday that I gave birth."

"Yeah, time seems to be flying by," he agrees then tips his head to the side. "Go shower, baby."

"Right." I turn and head down the hall then check on Jenna before I get into the shower. Dressed and waiting in the living room forty minutes later, I jump slightly when there's a knock on the door.

"It's going to be okay," Justin reassures me with a quick kiss before he opens the door.

"There's my baby boy!" His mom tackles him with a hug before she even makes it all the way into his apartment, and I smile at how tiny she is in comparison to him.

"Mom." He bends to kiss her cheek, and her eyes lock on mine.

"And you must be Aubrey!" She leaves his side and rushes toward me, wrapping me in a tight hug. "Look at how gorgeous you are." She leans back to study me then shakes her head. "No wonder my boy is so smitten."

"Jesus, Mom," he grumbles, and his dad claps him on his back and chuckles.

"Don't act so surprised. You know how she is."

"Maybe, but I wasn't expecting her to practically attack her." He shuts the door and moves close, wrapping his arm around me. "She's still recovering from having Jenna."

"Stop. I'm fine." I look up at him, leaning into his side, and I swear I hear his mom sigh.

"I can't wait to meet your baby girl," his mom says, gaining my attention. "But first, since my son seems to have forgotten his manners, I'll introduce myself. I'm Cora, and this is my husband Jasper."

"Sorry, Mom."

I smile at how quickly he apologizes and wonder if he's had a lot of practice doing that.

"Cut the boy some slack, Cora. I'm sure he isn't getting much sleep, and he's probably wondering if we'll be on our best behavior around his girl or if we'll do our best to embarrass him," Jasper says, setting two large tote bags on the kitchen counter before turning our way.

"Oh!" Cora grins at her husband. "You should've reminded me to tuck one of his baby albums into the bag. Then Aubrey could've seen how adorable he was when he played pirate in the bath—"

"Jenna is in the bedroom, Mom," Justin cuts her off. "She should be waking up any minute now to eat, if you want to go check on her."

"Ooh, can I?" She turns to me, and I nod. I follow her into the bedroom and smile as she lifts Jenna, who's blinking her eyes open, out of the bassinet. "It looks like I have perfect timing."

"She's on a pretty set schedule now. I swear she wants to eat every hour and a half. She'd probably eat more if I fed her."

"I remember those days. They lasted a long time with Justin, since he was such a greedy little boy." She heads toward the recliner in the corner of the room that Justin had delivered yesterday. "Do you mind if I sit with her for a minute?"

"Not at all. I'll be back in a minute to change her diaper and feed her. I'm just going to grab the stuff from the living room."

"Take your time." She doesn't even bother looking at me and I smile. I head into the kitchen to grab a glass of water, since I always get thirsty when I breastfeed, but Justin's already poured one for me.

"You doing okay, sweetheart?" he asks, wrapping his arms around my waist from behind.

"Yeah," I whisper back. "It's not as bad as I thought." I blush when I hear his dad's deep chuckle behind me. "Sorry." I turn to face him. "That sounded worse than I meant it."

"No apology needed, Aubrey. I'm not offended at all—more the opposite, actually. I wouldn't have liked you half as much for our boy if you weren't at least a little worried about meeting his parents."

"Well then, you should like me a ton, because the only reason I'm not a nervous wreck is because I didn't have enough time to get all worked up about your visit," I say, and he smiles right as Jenna's hungry cry rings through the air. "Duty calls."

I hurry back to the bedroom and hear Jasper say, "You did good, son. Pretty and sweet is a hard combination to find."

It feels good to get the stamp of approval from Justin's dad, and judging by the smile on Cora's face when she hands Jenna over to me before she leaves the room, I figure I have it from her too. I feel like a weight has been lifted from my shoulders, and I'm much more relaxed when Jenna and I join everyone in the living room, where I discover Justin was right about his mom bringing over a ton of food.

I settle on a roast beef sandwich and chips, and while I eat, Jenna falls asleep in Cora's arms.

Twenty minutes later, she stands and hands Jenna over to Justin, announcing, "We're going to go so Aubrey can take a nap. The best advice I can give you, honey, is to sleep whenever Jenna does. It's the only way you won't feel exhausted all the time."

"I'll try to remember to do that," I say, and she smiles, walking toward me, and I stand to give her a hug.

"I'm just a phone call away if you have questions or if you just need me to come over so you can have a break."

"Thank you." My arms tighten around her and my eyes fill with tears. I pull in a deep breath to get myself under control, more thankful than she could ever know for her offer. I always expected to have my mom at my side to offer advice or just to lean on when I had my first child, and it's difficult when I remember she's not around.

Once they leave, I head into the bedroom for a much-needed nap, and it doesn't take me long at all to fall asleep. A half an hour later, I hear Justin's deep rumble in the other room, and since Jenna is still asleep, I start to roll over to try to go back to sleep, but stop and jerk upright when I hear Jenna's father's name come out of Justin's mouth.

Chapter 12

Justin

"THIS ISN'T GOING to be good. Paulie Sr. isn't stupid. He's going to figure out that Kai coming back to life is connected to his son dying," I tell Kenton, knowing something is going to have to be done about Paulie Sr. sooner rather than later.

"Paulie Jr. is dead?"

I'm so focused on delivering my warning to Kenton that I don't realize Aubrey is awake, let alone in the room. My head jerks around at her question, just in time to spot her fall to the floor like her legs gave out. I disconnect the call without a word and drop my phone as I rush to her side. I pick her up and place her on the couch then kneel on the ground next to her. "Shit, Aubrey. Are you okay? Should I take you to the hospital?"

Her skin is so pale it's almost see-through, but her hold is strong when she grabs my hand and squeezes hard enough to cause pain. "Who were you on the phone with? Why were you talking about Paulie Jr.? How do you know him? Did you tell anyone in Vegas we're here?"

"Paulie Jr.?"

"Yes!" she shrieks, stunning me by grabbing my shoulders. "Did you tell anyone I'm here?"

"Baby, Jesus." The pieces click together and it hits me.

I've already killed the motherfucker who raped her.

I'm not sure I'll ever be able to tell her. I never want her to look at me with the same fear she has in her pretty blue eyes right now, but knowing he's dead and can't hurt her or anyone else fills me with relief.

"Breathe for me," I say quietly, knowing I need to be extra careful explaining the situation to her. "I was on the phone with Kenton. We were talking about Paulie Jr., because one of our friends has been having some trouble with his dad, and he needed our help."

"You helped Paulie Jr.? Was he a friend of yours?" She jerks away from me, sounding horrified.

"Of course not, sweetheart." I get up and take a seat on the couch with her then resituate her on my lap so I can see and hold her while we talk. "Paulie Jr. was going after the wife of one of my friends. She inherited some property in Vegas, and he wanted it for himself. He thought if he had control over it, it would give him the power he needed to get out from under his father's thumb and take his dad's seat."

"Were you guys able to help her before he"—she pauses and shivers before continuing on—"did anything to hurt her?"

She doesn't use the actual word, but I get what she's trying to ask. I rush to reassure her. "His goal was to marry her, but he never got close enough to try anything with her. Kai, her husband, and his team were set to confront him in a club in Vegas, but a sniper took him out before they got the chance." I skip the part about me being the one who pulled the trigger. Maybe I'll tell her about it someday, when we're happily married and I don't need to worry about the possibility of it sending her running in the opposite direction.

"He's really dead?" Her voice is just above a whisper.

"I saw his body myself," I assure her, and she melts against me. "Is his dad the reason you can't go back? Does Paulie Sr. know about Jenna? Is he the one looking for you?"

Her head jerks back and her blue eyes scan mine. "I don't think anyone knows about Jenna besides my family."

"Fuck."

"Why? Did you hear something? Is he looking for me?"

"Don't get pissed, but I started digging into your past when I brought you and Jenna home from the hospital. A couple nights ago, I came across a chat where someone mentioned your name and said they were looking for you."

"Who was it?"

"I don't know. I haven't been able to find out."

"Did they say where to call if I was found?"

"Baby, the dark web doesn't work like that. It's all codes and shit. I'm still working on figuring out who it is," I explain, and her body stiffens like she's preparing to jump off my lap, so my arms tighten around her.

"I will never let anyone hurt you or get to Jenna. You have to trust me."

"You went behind my back and dug into my past."

"Yeah, to protect you. I didn't know who hurt you, baby, and I wanted to make sure I was prepared in case he ever came after you or Jenna." Had I known I already killed him, I wouldn't have started the search... but then again, I wouldn't have discovered someone's been actively looking for her.

"The reason my brother pushed so hard for me to get an abortion was because he didn't want word to get out about who the father was. The only people who knew were him and my parents. I didn't tell any of my friends. I didn't go to the doctor to confirm the over-the-counter test I took was accurate."

"Your brother wanted to protect you and didn't see Jenna as a person." Her only response is a nod. "He figured the easiest way to reduce the risk of Paulie Sr. or his son coming after you was for you to get an abortion."

"Yeah," she whispers. "But I couldn't do it. She's been a person to me from the moment I saw the plus sign on the test, and I've loved her every minute since then."

"That's part of what makes you so fucking special, Aubrey. You were in an impossible situation. Nobody would've blamed you for doing what your brother asked, but you took the hard route to protect the innocent life growing inside you." It's also a big part of why I fell in love with her so quickly, but now isn't the right time to tell her. Not with what we're talking about. I also don't think she's ready to hear me confess my feelings yet. It'll have to wait for another day. Soon though. I'm not sure I can hold out much longer.

She rests her head against my shoulder and I kiss her forehead. "Do you think you can find out who's been looking for me?"

"Of course I can. I've already got a trace running. It's just a matter of time before it picks something up."

"If it's that easy for you, will it be that easy for someone else to find me?"

"No, they should hit a dead end if they search the hospital records. I switched your address and mangled your information in their records so nobody can use it to track you down."

"What about my doctor? Can they track me through him?"

I shake my head. "I changed everything, so don't freak out when it's wrong at your next visit."

"What about my bills? I won't get them if they go to the wrong place."

"I've already paid them off." I tighten my hold on her again, but it turns out not to be necessary, because she doesn't get pissed.

"You moved all of Jenna's stuff in here before asking me if I wanted to move in with you, bought her everything she could possibly need, and covered my bills before talking to me about it." She shakes her head. "You're almost as high-handed as Aedan, but in a good way."

"Aedan?"

Her smile disappears. "My brother."

Her bossy big brother who's probably worried about his little sister. "Do you think Aedan could be the one looking for you?"

She tilts her head to the side and considers the possibility for a moment before nodding. "I guess it could be him. I didn't tell anyone I was leaving or where I was going, which I'm sure drove him nuts when they discovered I was gone. I wouldn't put it past him to still be searching for me after all this time. Aedan can be pretty relentless. It's part of what helped him move up so quickly in the drug business."

"The drug business?"

Her eyes leave mine and I can see she's uncomfortable. "Yeah, he was only twenty-three when he killed his boss and made a name for himself. But not just because he wanted his job," she assures me like it makes it better. "The guy was a total creep when it came to women, kidnapping them and getting them hooked on drugs before pimping them out. Aedan might be a drug dealer, but what his boss was doing was unacceptable to him. Since nobody else would do anything to stop the guy and he was in a position to take care of it, he killed him."

"You got a phone number I can use to get ahold of him?"

"Yeah, but…" She looks away. "I don't want him to be able to trace me."

"That's where my super-secret spy skills come in handy," I say and she laughs. I give her a quick kiss then shift her off my lap and go to my desk, grabbing one of my burner phones from the bottom drawer. "This has no GPS, and the number isn't connected to me. We can call him on this without any risk of him finding you."

She eyes the phone warily. "I'm not sure I'm ready to talk to him yet. It's too soon after Jenna's birth, and all I can think about is how she wouldn't be here if I listened to him."

"You don't need to talk to him." I sit down next to her and take her hand. "I'll call him; all I need to know is if he's the one looking for you."

"Okay." She takes the phone from me, flips it open, and punches in a number before handing it back. I squeeze her hand then press the green button and put the phone to my ear, listening to it ring.

"O'Sullivan."

"Aedan O'Sullivan?"

"Yeah, you got him. Who the fuck is this?"

I get up and pace back and forth in front of the couch. "Who I am doesn't matter as much as who's sitting in front of me."

"Aubrey. You have my sister? I swear to fucking God, if you lay a single finger on her, I'll hunt you down and make you wish I'd kill you, motherfucker."

He's loud enough that Aubrey flinches. "Keep it down, asshole. You're scaring your sister."

"Scaring her?" His tone ratchets down to a whisper. "Who the fuck are you?"

"I'm the man she and her daughter are living with." It's as much as I'm willing to tell him until I can figure out for myself if he can be trusted with Aubrey and Jenna's whereabouts.

"She had a girl?"

The pain in his voice is enough to make me stop pacing, and I sit down on the edge of the couch. "Yeah. They're both doing really good too."

"Then you need to keep who she is to yourself so they stay that way. There are people here who would kill to get their hands on that baby."

"That's why I'm calling. I picked up a trace on her online, and I'm working to track down the source."

"As far as I know, I'm the only one who's been looking for her. But if word gets out that she had a baby, questions will be asked." There's a loud crashing noise in the background, and it sounds an awful lot like he's just thrown something against the wall. "I don't like the idea of my baby sister living with some guy I've never met, but it's a fuck of a lot better than visiting her grave while some depraved asshole raises my niece. It's better if she stays out of the picture so people don't start to ask questions."

"I'm not going to let Paulie Sr. find out about her or the baby."

"How are you connected to the Amidio family?" he asks, his tone deadly.

He sure as fuck doesn't need to know I'm the one who killed Paulie Jr., so I toss out two names that'll let him know I'm playing for the opposite side without giving too much away. "Kai and Sven."

"Well, fuck," he groans. "Seems we all have the same problem then."

"Yeah," I agree, "and I think we might be able to help each other out with it."

"As long as you understand Aubrey is never coming back and doesn't exist as far as anybody in Vegas is concerned, I'll be more than willing to work with you."

I'm irritated the bastard still seems to think he has a say in what Aubrey does. "Considering I have no intention of letting her leave my side and I want her safe, that works for me."

"I'm gonna need to hear that from my sister before we talk any further," he growls.

"You want to talk to your sister." Aubrey's eyes go wide, and she shakes her head. "You're gonna have to give me a second to talk to her.

She's not exactly a fan of yours right now, and I can't say I blame her."

"Let me talk to my sister," he barks.

My hand tightens around the phone. "Let me make one thing clear. She and her daughter are mine to take care of and protect, so if she doesn't want to speak to you, I'm not going to force her."

"Motherfucker, put—"

I don't hear more, because she grabs the phone out of my hand and hisses, "I'm fine. Your niece is fine. And if you fuck over Justin, I'll track you down and castrate you." She shoves the phone back at me then disappears down the hall.

"I need to make a few phone calls, but I'll be in touch," I say when I put the phone back to my ear.

"Is she really okay? Is my niece all right?"

"They are both fine. We'll talk soon." I hang up when Aubrey comes back down the hall carrying Jenna.

"It sounds like you plan on helping my brother with something."

"Yeah," I agree, not wanting her to know too much.

She chews the inside of her cheek, looking away as she takes a seat on the couch. "Can you make me a promise?"

"It depends." I won't promise her that I'm not going to do whatever I need to do to make sure she and Jenna are protected, and unfortunately, some of the things I might need to do probably won't make her happy.

"Just promise me that no matter what my brother pulls you into, you'll always be the kind of man Jenna can look up to. That you won't stop being the man I'm falling in love with."

"The only thing that will change is my ability to sleep without worrying something could harm either of my girls," I tell her, and she studies me for a long moment before nodding.

Chapter 13

Aubrey

"YOUR TURN," I urge, rolling over in the bed with the phone in my hand and Justin's face on the screen.

"You're going to make me give up all my secrets, aren't you?"

"You're the one who wanted to play this game," I remind him.

"You're a heartless little thing." He flashes me a sexy grin. "I like it."

"When it comes to you being a man of mystery? Yup!" I grin back at him. "But it's only fair, since I lost any chance at being a woman of mystery when you came into the labor and delivery room with me after we'd only known each other a couple of weeks."

"When you put it that way, you have an excellent point," he grumbles. "You already know what I do for Kenton, but I have a group of online hackers and activists I lead separate from the work I do with him."

"You mean like Anonymous?" I don't know much—or anything really—about hacking, but pretty much everyone has heard about the infamous hacktivist group on the news.

"Generally speaking? Sure," he admits reluctantly. "But our goals are very different. We help shut down terrorists and extremists by hacking their websites."

My eyes widen in surprise, because it sounds like his group is into some serious stuff. "So do I need to worry about the FBI breaking down your door in the middle of the night because of whatever it is that you do with your hacker friends?"

"You don't have anything to worry about. I'm more likely to work with the authorities than have them hunt me down." He runs a hand over the beard he's been growing out since I gave birth to Jenna. "Under the table, of course. The shit I do is in no way legal, but there are some people high up in the legal system who see the value in having someone who can go where they can't."

"Do you guys have a cool name? Because I'll be even more impressed if you do."

His grin turns sheepish. "Yeah, we're called the Winds of the North."

"I love it."

"All right, baby, time for you to go to sleep." He smiles, and I touch the screen of my phone with one finger.

"I miss you."

"I miss you too, but I'll be home tomorrow morning."

"Good." I sigh then sit up when Jenna starts to cry. "I need to feed her."

"I miss being there for that," he says, and my cheeks warm thinking about the times I breastfed with him holding me. "Kiss my girl, tell her I love her, and I'll see you soon."

"Okay, night."

"Night, baby." He hangs up, and I click off my phone then gather my girl and feed her one more time before putting us both to bed for the night.

"How is it that you always manage to find the coolest toys for her?" I ask Justin, watching him the next afternoon as he sets up an infant-to-toddler rocker seat in the middle of the living room while Jenna sleeps in the next room.

"It's amazing what you can find on the Internet when you look." He glances up at me, and his crystal-blue eyes twinkle with humor. God, I love his eyes. Really, I love *him*. Over the last six weeks, that's become glaringly clear. Even when he's away doing whatever it is he's doing in Vegas with my brother, he's made sure to stay connected to me and Jenna with video calls. He says he doesn't want to miss out on one

76

second of our girl growing up—something that is definitely possible. Jenna is still eating all the time, and I'm still exhausted, but it's all worth it. She's already gained three pounds, is holding up her head, and smiles all the time. She's also just as in love as I am with the man a few feet from me.

"Won't you get teased by all your hacker friends if they check your browser history and see you're searching for baby toys all the time?" I joke.

"Nah." He shakes his head, getting up on his knees and moving to where I'm sitting to loom over me. "I'm smart enough to wipe those searches so nobody can find 'em." He kisses me, and I slide my fingers into his hair, getting lost in his kiss. When he pulls away, I feel disappointed like I always do.

"Can I ask you something?"

"Anything." He smiles, touching his lips to mine softly.

"What're you doing with me?" I wave my hand in the air between us. "You're hot, smart, and sweet. You could have any girl you want."

He rests his forehead against mine and stares into my eyes. "I don't want any girl but you. Don't you get it? You and Jenna are everything to me."

I shake my head and stand up, forcing him back, then walk to the window and stare out at the parking lot. "You've spent the past two months proving that to me."

"You're saying that, but I'm getting the feeling it's not a compliment." He wraps his arms around me from behind and rests his chin on my shoulder. "Where is all this coming from?"

"The doctor cleared me at my appointment today."

"Cleared you?"

"You know, *cleared me*." I turn in his arms and look into his blue eyes that don't hold even the tiniest speck of understanding. My cheeks fill with heat as I murmur, "She told me it was okay for me to resume normal sexual activity."

He takes a small step back and slides his palms down my arms to grip my hands. "It doesn't matter what your doctor says. We're never going to do anything you're not one hundred percent ready for. I'm in no rush,

Aubrey."

"Don't you want to have sex with me?"

"Baby."

"You always stop when things between us heat up," I point out on a whisper.

"You just had Jenna, and your past…." He stops to shake his head. "I want things to happen when you're ready for them to happen."

"I'm ready. I've been ready. I just… I just want to know that you want to be with me like that."

"Jesus, you're crazy," he says, and I blink at him.

"What?"

"Have you honestly doubted that I want to be with you, that I want to fuck you?"

"I—"

"Aubrey, all I have to do is see you to get hard. I want you; never doubt that. I just never want to push you into something you're not ready for." He shakes his head. "I can't believe we're having this fucking conversation. I'm obsessed with you, infatuated with you, in love with you. I want to fuck you, make love to you, eat you, take you in every position possible. You're everything I ever wanted and more, and if you tell me you're ready to go there, I'm ready for it too."

Chapter 14

Justin

"YOU LOVE ME?" Her pretty blue eyes fill with tears and I pull her against my chest.

"Yes, I love you. The moment I saw you the first time, I was infatuated, and then I met you and knew you were the one I'd been waiting for. The only question is... do you love me too?" I brace for her answer, unsure if she's ready to admit to either of us how she feels about me.

"Of course I do. How could I not? You've made it impossible not to fall head-over-heels."

"I want to hear you actually say it."

"Say what?" she asks with a small smile.

"You know what." I lift her off her feet and carry her to the couch, laying her down.

"I love your beard."

"Keep going." I kiss down her neck.

"I love your body."

"More." I slide my hands up her shirt and pull it up over her head, finding her without a bra—something she hasn't put on yet today.

"I love your mouth." She hisses as I pull one of her nipples into my mouth, "Justin."

"I'm here," I groan, my need to claim her for my own almost

unbearable. Knowing she's medically cleared to have sex doesn't help my control. The urge to have her has been growing from the moment I first set eyes on her.

"I love *you*," she says as I kiss down her stomach, and I look up at her, meeting her gaze.

"I want this to be your choice. I want you to want this." I scoot up and settle between her legs.

"The only thing I've been able to think about since I walked out of the doctor's office is having sex with you. Then Jenna went down for her nap and you were doing something to make her life better like you always do, which just made you even sexier than usual. And I—"

I press my index finger against her lips to stem the flow of her nervous chatter. "Are you telling me that all the drama earlier was because you want to have sex?"

Her eyes narrow. "There wasn't drama."

"Baby." My cock hardens and presses against the zipper of my jeans at the thought of finally being able to sink inside her wet heat.

"I changed my mind." She tries to get up, but I hold her down.

"Oh no." I slide my hand under her chin so I don't lose sight of her eyes. "I always want you to have everything you need. So tell me, baby, do you want my cock?"

She licks her lips, her eyes dropping to my mouth, and I groan. "Yes." Her plump lips form a perfect circle, and it makes me think about how they'd look wrapped around my hard length.

I grind my hips against her and say, "I'm ready, willing, and able whenever and wherever you want me."

Her gaze darts to the bedroom door, which is fully shut, and then over to the monitor screen on the coffee table in front of the couch. Jenna is sleeping soundly in her bassinet, where I laid her down about half an hour ago. Aubrey's cheeks are a deep pink color when she turns back to me and blurts out, "We have anywhere from another minute to three hours before she wakes up. Is that enough time?"

My control slips another notch at her boldness. I slide my hands under her ass to lift her up and against me, and her legs circle my hips. The couch is not the ideal location for her first time, but we have to work

80

with what we've got since we have Jenna. "It isn't very manly of me to admit it, but one minute will probably be plenty of time for me, since my cock feels like it's gonna explode just from hearing you talk about us having sex."

"Really?" Her smile is one of feminine satisfaction as I lower my head.

"Yeah," I breathe into her ear, enjoying her little shiver in reaction. "But let's hope for at least five minutes, so I can get you off first."

Her hands slip beneath the back of my shirt, her nails scraping along my skin as she moans, "Uh-huh."

I suck the lobe of her ear into my mouth and bite it gently. She moans and squirms restlessly beneath me as I start to kiss my way down her body. Her back arcs off the cushions, and I cup her perfect tits, listening to her sigh. I nibble and suck my way around them and tweak the hard, pink little peaks at the tips with my teeth. She writhes when I slide down her body and tug her soft, black cotton pants and panties down her legs.

The scent of her desire hits me and I groan. "I've missed your pussy so fucking much, sweetheart." I use two fingers to spread her lips wide then lick up the center and circle my tongue around her clit before pulling it into my mouth with a little tug. Her hips jerk up and her fingers dig into my scalp. "I could spend those three hours right here and still not get my fill of you."

Her body starts shaking, and I pull away to look up at her. With my eyes locked on hers, I breathe against her core and scrape my beard along the sensitive skin of her inner thighs. Her eyes grow wide while her body goes taut, and her hips buck up against my mouth. I suck at her, plunging my tongue as deep as it can go until she screams out my name and shudders from her orgasm. Then I lick her through it until her body relaxes again. I press my cock into the cushions, and a deep growl rumbles up my chest.

Her long eyelashes flutter and her eyes open. "Did I do something wrong?"

"No, sweetheart, you did everything right letting yourself go like that for me," I reassure her.

"But you sound like you're in pain."

"I wouldn't call it pain." I rise up on my knees and unbutton my jeans. "Just at the end of my control."

"Oh." Her gaze drops to my zipper, and her eyes go half-mast.

My cock feels like it's ready to bust through my jeans to get to her, so I shove my pants down to my knees and kick them off. My hard cock bounces free and I settle over her, my crown almost touching her heat when I realize I'm forgetting something important. "Shit, I need to grab a condom."

"Um... you don't have to use one if you don't want to." She grabs my biceps to stop me from moving away. "The doctor said the chances of me getting pregnant are almost zero during the next month or so while I'm breastfeeding."

"You okay with me taking you bare?" I hold myself still, waiting for her answer when my body is urging me to thrust inside her until I'm balls-deep.

"I want to feel you moving inside me without anything between us."

"Fuck." I claim her mouth in a deep kiss. "You keep talking like that and we'll be lucky if I last a second, let alone a minute."

Her plump lips curve up at the edges, and she twines her arms around my neck. "Then how about we stop talking?"

I can see a hint of fear in her eyes. I press a gentle kiss against her lips, because the last thing I want to do is scare her. I pour all my love for her into it as my tongue duels with hers while we both drown in sensual need. My cock nudges her entrance, and she shudders. "Are you sure you're ready for this?"

"That depends. Does it bother you that I don't have a clue what I'm doing?" she asks.

"It doesn't bother me at all. It's the opposite actually."

"What do you mean?"

"Men can be territorial over their women. I've never experienced it before, but everything is different with you." I slide the head of my cock through her wetness then slowly sink inside her, watching her eyes drift shut. "Keep your eyes on mine, sweetheart." When I'm finally anchored deep inside her, I don't see anything but pleasure in her gaze. "Fuck. It's wetter, hotter, and even better than I dreamed," I grunt. "Your pussy is wrapped so tight around me."

"Justin." Her nails dig into my back. I've waited so long for this moment. I know I won't be able to hold back the release I already feel building inside me for long, but I'm determined to make this good for her. To get her to fly apart for me before I let go. I pump in and out of her, slowly at first, waiting to make sure she can handle me before picking up the pace. Burying my face in her neck, I try to control the urge to come.

My hips continue to thrust back and forth as I slide my hand between our bodies to circle her clit with my thumb. Her pretty blue eyes stay locked on mine, and I watch as it builds for her until she falls over the edge. Her full breasts thrust forward when her back arches, and her nails dig into my back. "I've never seen anything as beautiful as you are like this."

Her legs grip my waist and I brace my feet against the arm of the couch to give myself the added leverage I need as my thrusts speed up. Her pussy convulses around me, milking my orgasm from me and her walls clamp down around my cock as we both come.

After the shudders subside and we both catch our breath, I roll us over so she's sprawled on top of me and hold her close, feeling like I'm holding the entire world in my arms.

Chapter 15

Aubrey

"MARRY ME."

I look up from Jenna, who just finished feeding, and is now asleep, shaking my head at Justin leaning with his shoulder against the doorjamb and watching us. "What?"

"Marry me," he repeats, and I laugh thinking he's joking. He walks across the room toward me and gets down on his knees at the side of the bed. "I'm serious, Aubrey." He takes my hand as he pulls a ring box from the pocket of his sweats, flipping it open.

"You're serious?" My breath catches as he lifts a gorgeous princess-cut diamond ring from its velvet bed. "You want to marry me?"

"I want to spend the rest of my life with you, and if you're okay with it, I'd like to adopt Jenna, so you'll both have my last name."

Tears fill my eyes and begin to drip down my cheeks. "Yes," I whisper, unable to get out any more than that one word. When I left Vegas, my family, and everything I ever knew, I didn't dare to dream of having a family again. I never once thought I'd find the perfect man for me or an amazing father for Jenna.

"I don't want to put this off, baby," he says, sliding the ring on my finger. "I want you to be my wife sooner rather than later. We can get married now and plan a big party when things settle down."

"How soon?"

"Today, tomorrow." He shrugs. "All it'll take is a quick trip to the county clerk's office to get our marriage license. There's no waiting period, so we can get married as soon as we have it. And my dad knows a judge who'll do it for us."

"That is really soon," I say, a niggle of worry in the back of my mind. "Why?"

He looks at Jenna then at the ring on my finger, and even though I can't see his eyes, I can tell he's tense. "I have to go back to Vegas."

My heart sinks thinking about him being away from us again. "When?"

"Sven will send a plane when I tell him I'm ready to go."

I haven't met any of Justin's friends other than Kenton and Autumn, but I know Sven is involved in everything that's going down in Vegas. Well, him and another guy named Kai.

I look at the beautiful ring on my finger and my throat gets tight. Even when I've asked, he hasn't talked to me about what's been happening. All he's said is things are being taken care of. Still, I have a feeling it's worse than he's been letting on. It could also be why he's pushing so hard for me to marry him now.

"Are you worried about what might happen while you're away? Is it why you want to marry me?"

"I want to marry you, because I'm in love with you and want to spend the rest of my life as your husband and Jenna's father." He cups my cheeks. "Do you trust me?"

I don't even have to think about that answer. "With my life and Jenna's."

"Do you love me?" His fingers skim down my cheek.

"You know I do."

He places his lips against mine. "Do you want to spend the rest of your life with me?"

"Yes."

He takes my hand and his thumb caresses the skin on my finger just under his ring. "Then just trust me."

I close my eyes and remind myself that he's always done everything within his power to take care of Jenna and me and that he would never do anything to hurt us. "Okay." I open my eyes back up.

"Thank you." He kisses me swiftly then stands and takes Jenna from my arms and places her in her bassinet. When he comes back to me, he pulls out his phone, dialing before putting it on speaker. "She said yes!"

"Of course she did," I hear who I think is Jasper say, and my eyes widen. "Congratulations, son."

"Thanks, Dad."

"Yep, hold on. Your mom's been waiting for you to call."

"I'm so excited," Cora says, and Justin grins at me, making me wonder when he spoke to his parents about his plan and exactly how much they know.

"Good, because I need your help."

"Whatever you need."

"I'm gonna take care of Jenna while you take Aubrey out to look for a dress."

"I'm on my way," she says then adds, "I should be there in the next thirty minutes."

He laughs while I just stare at him. "Thanks, Mom."

"You're welcome, honey." The line goes dead.

"How long have you been planning this exactly?" I ask as he lifts me up then settles me on his lap.

"I've had your ring for the last three weeks. I wanted to ask you when you were comfortable being away from Jenna for a night or two, but this afternoon, I...." He shakes his head. "It doesn't matter. Things changed, and I don't want to leave again without you being my wife."

"Will things ever be normal between us?" I ask, resting my head on his shoulder.

"Normal?"

I tip my head back to catch his eye. "You met me when I was pregnant. We haven't even had a real date, because I gave birth not long after we met. Jenna and I moved in with you just days after she was born—something you knew would happen, because you moved us in without even asking me beforehand," I remind him, and he smiles at the memory. "Now we're getting married, but doing it within a few hours of you asking me." My nose wrinkles. "We're totally not normal."

"I like how things are between us. We skipped all the bullshit and got right to the good stuff."

"Still, we're not normal."

"I'm okay with that." He kisses me then lifts me off his lap to stand. "Now go get ready, so you can pick out your wedding dress."

"Do I even need a dress if we're just going to the courthouse?"

"Yes," he says firmly with a twinkle in his eye that makes me wonder if he's up to something.

"I'm trusting you."

"I know, baby, and I'm so fucking lucky." He kisses me swiftly and then spins me toward the bathroom. I hurry to get ready, but even so, by the time I'm done, Cora is waiting for me.

I love you, Justin mouths, and I hold back tears as he takes Jenna from my arms and rests her on his chest.

Justin once again proved he's capable of making miracles happen. In the twenty-four hours since he asked me to marry him, he's somehow given me a little bit of normal. Under an arch of flowers, holding a bouquet of cream roses in his parents' backyard, I'm marrying the man of my dreams with his parents and mine as our witnesses.

I was shocked last night when Justin told me we were going to dinner and I walked into the restaurant to find my parents waiting for us. Not surprisingly, Justin won over both my mom and dad without trying, but I have to admit I was a little astonished with the way they fawned over Jenna. It feels right to have them here today, but even with them, the judge marrying us, Jasper, and Cora here, I still feel like it's just me, my soon-to-be husband, and our girl.

He looks gorgeous in his black suit, white dress shirt, and baby-pink tie that matches Jenna's frilly dress, the silk ribbon around my waist and stem of my flowers, and I feel prettier than I have in a long time. Cora and my mom helped me get ready. His mom curled my hair and mine did my makeup, and each of them gave me my something borrowed and something blue. Luckily, even with short notice, I found the perfect dress—a simple white lace gown with an empire waist and small pearls sewn into the material around the neckline.

I can't tear my gaze off his when the judge starts to speak, and tears I can't hold back stream down my cheeks as we exchange our vows. When it's time for us to exchange rings, he hands Jenna over to his dad and pulls two platinum bands from his jacket pocket. A perfect match for each other, his is a wider version of the one that goes with the engagement ring already on my finger.

"These rings are a symbol of your commitment to your marriage, a reminder of who you are, where you've been, and where you're going," the judge says as we take each other's hand. "In giving and receiving these rings, you acknowledge that wherever you go, you will always return to your shared life together." Tears fill my eyes once more as we slide them onto each other's finger. "May your rings remind you that marriage is a journey, with no beginning and no end, just a moment-to-moment opportunity to love and be loved to the best of your ability."

He speaks some more; I know he does, but until he says "you may kiss the bride" and Justin takes my mouth, my mind is so overwhelmed with everything that's happened and I don't hear anything. When he finally pulls his lips from mine, we're married, but we still have drama to face before we start our life together.

"I don't like this," I tell Justin, watching him pull my suitcase out the back of his Rover and set it on the ground after hugging his parents and Jenna goodbye. It's only been a few days since we got married, and time that should have been spent with us enjoying being man and wife has been spent with my parents who left yesterday and Justin getting ready to go back to Vegas—something I wish he wasn't doing.

"I know, baby." He looks at his dad, who takes my bag while Cora carries Jenna into their house, where we will be staying while he's gone. He hasn't shared why he wants me with his mom and dad except to say this will be his longest trip and he wants me to have the help with Jenna. I don't believe him; I know there is more going on, but I don't want to stress him out by asking too many questions. Especially when I know us being with his parents has something to do with them protecting me and my girl. "This is my last trip. After I get back from Vegas, I'm never going back."

"I hate that you're leaving, especially now. This should be our honeymoon."

"Baby." He steps into my space, cupping my cheek with his palm. "When I get home, we'll go away, just you, me, and Jenna. I'll get us a place on a beach somewhere and we'll stay as long as you want." I shiver a little at the sensual promise in his gaze, and he smiles before touching his lips to mine. "I love you."

"I love you too." My throat gets tight. "Promise me you'll be safe while you're gone."

"I promise." He kisses me once more then glances at his watch. "I need to go. I'll call you."

I don't say a word. I watch him climb behind the wheel and start up the engine. I wrap my arms around my stomach as he pulls out of the driveway and stand there long after he disappears out of sight.

"Come inside, sweetie. It'll all be okay," Cora says, wrapping her arm around my waist. I let her lead me into the house and stop just inside when I catch sight of Jasper walking into the living room, carrying a rifle and a cleaning kit.

"If anyone tries to come for you, they're going to be in for one hell of a surprise." He sets both items on the coffee table and heads back into his office. When he comes out again, he has two more rifles.

My jaw drops, and I whisper, "How many guns does he have?"

Cora's voice is serious when she answers, "More than enough."

Lord, Justin better get home soon.

Chapter 16

Justin

"*I* CAN'T BELIEVE my sister married your ass and my parent actually like you," Aedan mutters as he pulls his car into the departure line at the airport.

"Get over it." I send a text to Aubrey to let her know I'm catching a flight home in the next hour and will be at my parents' to pick her up tonight. I did what I needed to do to make sure she's safe, and no one will ever know what happened to her. And after the paperwork I pushed through clears, Jenna will be officially mine, leaving no trace of her real father.

"I'd like to reconnect with my sister."

Fuck. "I don't know if I'm okay with that. I don't want my girls mixed up in your shit," I tell him, shoving my cell into the front pocket of my jeans.

Not only is Aedan a drug dealer, but he's now one of the biggest in the US after what happened.

"I want the chance to know my niece."

Anger curls up in my belly. If he would've had his way, there would be no Jenna, and I can't imagine a world without her in it.

"I know I fucked up. I know I did. I should have listened to Aubrey about keeping her. I know I should've figured something out, but I love my sister, and I know what could've happened to her if the truth came out about who Jenna's father was."

"I'm her father." I turn in my seat to face him. "If you ever get back into your sister's good graces, you need to understand that."

"Fuck, man." He jerks his fingers through his hair. "You're right."

I blow out a breath and attempt to get my temper under control before I say something I might regret. "Your sister loves you. Just give her time. Right now, all she's thinking about is Jenna not being here and why that would've been."

"I'll give her time. Just… fuck, please just talk to her. I miss her."

"I'll talk to her," I tell him, opening the door and getting out, unwilling to say more. Whatever happens between him and Aubrey will happen when she's ready, and not before then. I walk to the trunk, pound it with the back of my fist, and it pops open. I swing my duffle up over my shoulder then, without another look in his direction, I head into the airport to catch my flight home to both my girls.

"Is that how you greet visitors now?" I grin at my dad as he steps out onto the porch with a shotgun in his hand.

"All I saw were headlights. I didn't know who was here." He opens the door wide to let me through as he returns the gun to the case on the wall. "Glad you're home."

"Me too. Thanks for looking after my girls while I was away."

"You know I'm here anytime you need me." He pats my back as my eyes meet Aubrey's across the room.

"Hey." She smiles at me from the doorway of the kitchen.

I close the distance between us and wrap my arms around her, holding her close. "I missed you." I breathe in her scent, letting it wash away everything I saw and did.

"I missed you too."

It's been too long since I've held her, and I don't want to let her go, hating it when she releases me so my mom can hug me.

"As much as I've loved having Aubrey and Jenna here with us, I'm so glad to have you home safe." My mom gives me a look that asks a million questions, questions I'll never answer. I've told my dad some of what I've been doing the last few months, but even he doesn't know all the details.

"I'm happy to be home. I missed my girls." I look at Aubrey. "Where's Jenna?"

"Sleeping," she says then shakes her head when the baby cries. "She must know you're home."

"I'll get her and give you two a minute alone," Mom says, taking Dad's hand and pulling him out of the room.

I lead Aubrey over to the couch and sit down, pulling her onto my lap.

"Are you okay?" she asks, sliding her fingers through my hair as I wrap my arms around her waist and rest the side of my head on her chest.

"Oh yeah." I've kept my promise to her each and every trip, and this time isn't any different. "It's over."

"It's over?" she repeats on a whisper, and I tip my head back to look at her.

"Paulie's dead. His wife found out about his mistress and killed him. We didn't even have to get our hands dirty."

"So it's really over?"

"It is."

"My brother?"

"Still isn't my favorite person, but I don't dislike him as much as I did at first." She looks surprised by that. "He wants to reconnect with you and asked me to talk to you."

"I…" She shakes her head. "I don't know if I'm ready for that, if I'll ever be ready for that."

"You running marked him. He knows he messed up." I cup her cheek.

"He hurt me."

My jaw clenches. It kills me thinking of her in any kind of pain. Even her parents being in town for our wedding was hard on her, and I was tempted to send them back to Vegas sooner than planned. It was a catch twenty-two; she was happy they were here but still hurt by all that happened.

"I've got your back for whatever you decide, but I think it'd be good if you two spoke. He just wants you to be happy, even if it means he'll never be a part of your life again."

She leans into me and rests her head on my shoulder. "I don't know if I could ever trust him after what he did, after everything that's happened."

"This isn't something you need to decide on today, tomorrow, a year or however fucking long from now. The ball is in your court, baby."

"Thank you," she whispers, cupping my jaw. "Thank you for always putting me and Jenna first."

"No matter what, baby, you and Jenna will always be my priority," I say, knowing I'll work my ass off so she never regrets putting all her trust in me. She touches her lips to mine then smiles when Jenna cries. I turn my head and my chest warms when I see my baby girl's eyes on me. "Hey, pretty girl," I coo as Aubrey scoots off my lap, and I take Jenna from my mom. The minute she's in my arms, she latches onto the beard on my face, tugging hard enough I lean forward.

"You're probably going to need to shave that," Dad says, and I grin.

"Maybe I should shave my hair off too," Aubrey states, and I look at her, narrowing my eyes. "I'm kidding."

"You better be." I give her a swift kiss then lift my girl so we're eye-to-eye. "I missed you. Are you ready to go home?"

Her answer is to reach for my beard again, making me laugh.

"I'm gonna miss having the girls here," Mom says, eyeing the luggage and baby items packed up by the front door.

"Mom, we're less than thirty minutes away. You can come over whenever you want."

"I know." She waves me off. "It's just that Jenna has already gotten so big, and it feels like each day she grows more and more."

"I think that's how it works," I tell her, and she shakes her head.

"You and Aubrey should have another baby, so I don't run out of baby time."

"Why don't you let Aubrey and Justin decide when they are going to have more kids?" Dad suggests, rolling his eyes.

"It's their choice. I'm just saying I wouldn't be upset if they wanted to start now."

"I think you two should go." Dad grins at me. "If you don't, your mom might lock you in a room until she gets her way."

"Right." I stand with Jenna while chuckling at my mom, who's glaring at my dad. "We'll see you two in a few days."

"Don't worry, Cora. I'll try to convince your son," Aubrey says, surprising me, and I look at her. "What?" She shrugs. "I wouldn't mind having another sooner rather than later."

"Baby." Fuck, I want that. I want lots of babies with her.

"Yay!" Mom whispers loudly. "More babies."

I keep my eyes locked on Aubrey's then close them, wondering how the fuck I got so goddamn lucky.

Chapter 17

Aubrey

"*I* CAN'T BELIEVE we have a whole night to ourselves." I should probably be nervous about leaving Jenna, since it's my first time away from her, but I know she couldn't be in better hands. And I'm excited about spending the night alone with my husband.

"Mom and Dad will take good care of our girl," he assures me.

"I know they will." I lean into his side as we walk through the lobby. "This place is so cool."

"It used to be a train station."

"Really?"

"Yeah," he says as we stop at the elevator that will take us up to our suite.

"It's also haunted," a woman says, and I turn, meeting the eyes of an older lady with graying hair.

"Marsha, don't start," the man at her side, who's probably her husband, says, sounding exasperated.

"Well, it is."

"Really?" I ask her.

She nods, stepping closer to me, and Justin's body stiffens. I pat his abs to let him know it's okay. "They say a young girl named Abigail died here, throwing herself in front of a train after the love of her life didn't return from war. Now, she haunts the hotel and room 711."

"Oh my God," I whisper.

"I know." She takes my hand. "Isn't that so beautiful?"

I blink, not sure we have the same outlook on a woman dying because the man she loved didn't return from a horrible war. "Ummm...."

"Marsha." Her husband sighs.

"What?" She looks at him. "It's beautiful."

"Sorry, you two," her husband says, grabbing her arm and leading her away.

When the doors to the elevator open, I stand just outside the car as Justin steps in with our bag. "Babe."

"This place is haunted." I look around, expecting to see a ghost swoop down out of thin air to attack me. "We can't stay here."

"Jesus." He shakes his head, tugging my hand, and I stumble into the elevator car as he wraps his arm around my waist and holds me against him.

"Did you know this place is haunted?" I ask as the doors close and the elevator starts to rise.

"It's not haunted."

"That lady just said it was haunted."

"Sweetheart, it's not haunted."

"Are you sure?" I ask, and he looks away from me, not answering. "You knew it was haunted."

"It's just lore, baby, and it doesn't matter. We're not staying in room 711, and I don't expect you to see more than our room," he says as the doors open and he takes my hand. When we reach our room, he taps the key against the knob to unlock it then pushes the door in, gesturing for me to go inside.

As soon as the door shuts behind us, he drops our overnight bag on the floor and sweeps me off my feet. I barely get to see anything as he strides to the bedroom and tosses me on the king-sized bed. I laugh as he starts to strip off his clothes then moan as he makes quick work of mine. Once we're both completely naked, he comes down on top of me and presses me into the mattress.

His gorgeous blue eyes stay locked on mine as his hand slides down my neck and chest to toy with my nipples. As I writhe beneath him, he moves lower, his hand sliding down over my ribcage and belly to between my legs. When he reaches my pussy, he presses his palm against my clit, and my hips buck in response.

"Easy, sweetheart." He dips his head and drags his tongue over my clit. I whimper as he buries his face between my legs, his fingers entering me as he works me with his mouth. He doesn't relent; he licks and sucks until an orgasm rips through me, making me see stars. "I swear I'll never get enough of you."

"Then I guess it's a good thing I'm not going anywhere," I breathe, lifting up on my elbows to watch him wrap his hand around his cock and stroke his hard length.

"Spread your legs, baby. I want inside you."

I don't hesitate. I give him what he wants. I spread my legs as he slides the head of his cock through my wetness, and I glide my hands down his chest and trace the grooves of his abs. A deep groan rumbles from his chest, and I keep my eyes locked on his as he slowly enters me.

"Perfect. You're so fucking perfect for me."

I move my hand up his chest and wrap one around the back of his neck, pulling his head down so I can brush my lips against his. "I love you."

"I know." He thrusts into me hard and fast, going deeper and deeper with each powerful movement. Every time we make love is amazing, but this time feels different, like we're more connected than ever, heightening my senses, driving me closer to the edge faster than normal.

"I'm so close," I pant, my walls beginning to pulse around his hard length. My nails dig into his skin, my toes curling. When he releases his grip on my hips and glides his hands up to cup my breasts to pinch my nipple, it feels like there's a direct link to my core.

"Come for me, baby. I want to feel you come for me." His cock and his words send me over the edge, and my pussy clamps down on him while I scream his name. I hold onto him tighter as his hips ride me through my climax, and my nails dig into his back as he plants himself deep and finds his own release. When his weight rests against me, I close my eyes and soak in the feeling of us reconnecting, and I smile when I remember we have all night to just be Justin and Aubrey, a newlywed couple in love and starting a life together.

"I want a baby," he says, and I open my eyes as he pulls his head back to look me in the eye.

"Really?"

"I didn't have siblings. I want Jenna to have that. I want her to have brothers and sisters. I want a house full of kids driving us crazy."

Tears fill my eyes. "I want that too," I whisper right before he drops his mouth to mine to kiss me. Then, for the rest of the night, we work on making our dream a reality.

"Morning, baby." I open my eyes and see the man I love looming over me with a satisfied smile on his face.

"Morning." I stretch as he touches his lips to mine.

"Hungry?"

"Yes." I sit up, wondering how long he's been awake. Really, I expected us to sleep until noon, something neither of us has done since Jenna was born.

"I ordered room service. It should be here soon." He ogles my bare chest, and I roll my eyes as there is a knock on the door.

"Food's here." He stands up then asks, "Are you disappointed you didn't see a ghost last night?"

"Shut up." I toss a pillow at him as he walks across the room, listening to him laugh.

"It was just a question, baby." He grins at me as he comes back into view pushing a cart.

"Whatever." I eye the plates as he pulls off the lids, my mouth watering when I see a fluffy-looking omelet and fresh fruit.

"Can you check that for me?" he asks when his phone chimes on the table next to me.

"Sure." I frown when I see the name on the screen. "Why is Aedan sending you a message? I thought you were done with Vegas."

"Relax, baby." He takes the phone from my hand. "Just because your brother sent me a text doesn't mean shit's happening."

I narrow my eyes on him. "Why are you acting like it's no big deal Aedan's contacting you?"

"We talk at least once a week."

"You talk to him once a week?" I hiss, unsure how I feel about that.

"Yeah." He takes his phone and moves away from the bed, setting it down to pour a cup of coffee from the carafe on the tray.

"What do you talk about?"

"We don't talk. He normally just asks for photos or updates."

"Photos?"

"I send him pictures of Jenna," he says, bringing me a cup of coffee. I'm not sure how to react to the news that my husband and brother have been talking for the past few months without me knowing about it. A part of me is happy they're getting along, but another is pissed I didn't know.

"Why am I only hearing about this now?"

He shrugs his broad shoulders. "Because the last time we talked about your brother, you weren't ready to have anything to do with him."

"And you are?"

"I'm not saying I want to see him all the fucking time, but I feel for him, and he's not stepping on my toes. All he wants is to know you and Jenna are doing okay, so that's what I'm giving to him."

"Oh," I mutter.

"When you're ready, sweetheart, not before," he says, reading my mind.

I take a sip of coffee, wondering when that will be. I'm happier than I've ever been, and the only black cloud hanging over me is the pain of missing him. "Is it safe for him to be texting your regular phone and not a burner?"

"I wouldn't let him do it if it wasn't," he says quietly.

"So it's also safe to call him on it?"

"Yeah." He pushes the cart of food next to the bed and takes a seat next to me.

"Can I see your cell?" I ask, and his eyes search mine before he hands me the phone. I take it, and my hands tremble as I hold it.

"I'm right here." He touches his lips to my cheek, and I pull in the strength I need from him before I dial Aedan's number.

"What's going on? Are Aubrey and Jenna okay?" Aedan asks, and I close my eyes.

"We're fine," I whisper.

"Aubrey?"

"Yeah, it's me."

"Fuck, it's good to hear your voice," he rasps. "For a minute there, I thought something must've happened to you, because Justin never calls. He sticks to texts."

"Sorry for scaring you. Justin said it's safe to call, and I guess I figured I'd better do it now before I lose my nerve," I say as my husband takes my hand.

"You don't have to apologize. Not for anything. I'm the one who owes you an apology. I wish things were different. If I'd never gone down this path in the first place, things could have been—"

"Stop," I cut him off. "What happened to me isn't your fault. I wasn't targeted because of who you are. It was a case of me being in the wrong place at the wrong time, and the only person who's to blame is already dead. Let's leave it in the past where it belongs."

"Fine, I'll give you that." I listen to him let out a deep breath. "But I'm still so fucking sorry. I'm sorry I didn't listen to you, sorry that you ran, and sorry I'm missing out on knowing my niece."

This version of Aedan is very different from the one I left behind. And as much as I wish he'd been as open and understanding before, I'm glad he wasn't, because then I might never have met Justin.

"I accept your apology," I say, unsure what role I want him to play in our lives.

"Are you happy?" he asks, sounding curious.

"I have an amazing husband and a beautiful daughter," I whisper, closing my eyes. "Right now, I'm focusing on what I've gained instead of what I left behind."

"I'm happy for you, little sis."

"Thank you." I look at my husband, the man who changed everything for me, and know without a doubt my path led me exactly to where I needed to be.

Epilogue

"*I*T'S SO BEAUTIFUL here," Aubrey says, leaning back into me as Jenna plays in the sand a few feet away. The sunset casts a pink glow on the ocean and sky.

"It is." I kiss her temple, and she links her hand with mine and rests it on her stomach. "I have a feeling I can make it even better," I say, spotting the group of people coming down the beach toward us. I'm not surprised Aedan is wearing jeans and black motorcycle boots on a beach in Hawaii, since I've never seen him in anything else. Aaron and Alexander, Aubrey's other brothers, are dressed similarly, but her mom and dad look like they're ready for a luau, with colorful-printed clothes on and leis around their necks.

"Better than a Christmas Eve sunset on a private Hawaiian beach with you and Jenna? Not to mention your parents and friends in the house behind us, which looks like something from a magazine and is decorated for a television show." She looks at me over her shoulder. "I know you can pull off miracles, but I doubt you can do better than this."

I grin at her then take her chin between my fingers, kissing her before turning her head.

I don't see her face but still hear the tears in her voice as she whispers, "Aedan." She pushes up off the ground and races across the beach to throw herself into her brother's arms.

"Mama!" Jenna screeches, unsure what's happening.

"It's okay, baby." I pick her up and kiss her cheek then follow after Aubrey across the sand.

"My baby." Aubrey's mom stretches her hands out to Jenna, and I hand her over then look at Aubrey's dad when he pats me on the back.

"Thanks for making this happen."

"You don't need to thank me." I watch Aubrey hug Aedan then let him go to hug Aaron and Alexander. I couldn't think of a better way for us to spend Christmas than with friends and family in Hawaii, and it just happened to work out that Aedan was able to get away from Vegas for a few days.

"I can't believe you did this." Aubrey turns to face me with tears in her eyes. "Just when I think you can't get any better, you do something that proves I'll forever be trying to find ways to give you back even a little of what you give me."

"Baby, you give me everything."

She shakes her head. "I was going to wait to tell you tomorrow, but now seems like as good a time as any."

"Tell me what?"

"I'm pregnant."

"Fuck," Aedan mutters.

"You're pregnant?" I breathe.

"I took the test a couple days ago." She places her hands on her stomach. "I wanted to tell you tomorrow morning."

"You flew today." I shake my head, wondering if the long flight could harm the baby.

"It was a private plane, and your mom assured me when she helped me pack that it would be okay."

"My mom knew?"

"Yeah, she was going to watch Jenna tomorrow morning while I told you." She walks toward me and rests her hands on my chest. "This isn't exactly the reaction I expected."

"Bean, you just told the man you're having a baby. He's in shock like the rest of us are," Aedan says.

I don't take my eyes off Aubrey's, even when hers flash with mock annoyance in her brother's direction. "We're having another baby?" I wrap my hands around her hips.

"We're having another baby." She moves her hands up my chest to my shoulders, and I slide my hands down over her ass and lift her off the ground, watching her eyes light up as she smiles down at me.

"You say I'm capable of making miracles happen, baby, but pretty sure it's you who has that ability. Just when I think you've given me everything I want, you give me more," I say, and she leans her head down and presses her lips to mine.

With the Christmas dinner consumed, I walk into Kai and Myla's living room where Kenton, Kai, and Sven are watching the women play with the kids. Jenna and Maxim taking turns hammering away on a toy construction bench, while Aubrey hovers nearby. Myla rocking her baby girl in her arms while talking to Maggie, whose hand is covering her rounded belly.

We lucked out on the timing of this trip, because Maggie is due to have Sven's son, Maddox, in about six weeks. If it'd been even a couple weeks later, she wouldn't have been able to travel. The swell of Aubrey's belly isn't visible, but I love knowing she's carrying our son or daughter.

With Christmas music playing in the background, mixing with the sound of toddler chatter and the soft voices of our wives, I shake my head. It's hard to believe we all ended up here, considering what we all had to go through. But we fought hard for our slice of happiness, and now the only thing left to do is enjoy it.

ACKNOWLEDGMENTS

Thank you Rochelle Paige for holding my hand, making it possible to finally share Justin and Aubrey's story with the world. I don't know what I would do without your friendship, and support. I love you dear friend.

First I have to give thanks to God, because without him none of this would be possible. Second I want to thank my husband. I love you now and always—thank you for believing in me even when I don't always believe in myself. To my beautiful son, you bringing such joy into my life, and I'm so honored to be your mom.

To every blog and reader, thank you for taking the time to read and share my books. There would never be enough ink in the world to acknowledge you all, but I will forever be grateful to each and every one of you.

I started this writing journey after I fell in love with reading, like thousands of authors before me. I wanted to give people a place to escape where the stories were funny, sweet, and hot and left you feeling good. I have loved sharing my stories with you all, loved that I have helped people escape the real world, even for a moment.

I started writing for me and will continue writing for you. XOXO Aurora

ABOUT AURORA ROSE REYNOLDS

Aurora Rose Reynolds is a *New York Times* and *USA Today* bestselling author whose wildly popular series include Until, Until Him, Until Her, and Underground Kings.

Her writing career started in an attempt to get the outrageously alpha men who resided in her head to leave her alone and has blossomed into an opportunity to share her stories with readers all over the world.

OTHER BOOKS BY AURORA ROSE REYNOLDS

The Until Series
Until November
Until Trevor
Until Lilly
Until Nico
Second Chance Holiday

Underground Kings Series
Assumption
Obligation
Distraction

Until Her Series
Until July
Until June
Until Ashlyn
Until Harmony
Until December

Until Him Series
Until Jax
Until Sage
Until Cobi

Shooting Stars Series
Fighting to Breathe
Wide-Open Spaces
One last Wish

Fluke my life series
Running into love
Stumbling into love
Tossed into love
Drawn Into Love

Ruby Falls
Falling Fast

Alpha Law CA ROSE
Justified
Liability
Finders Keepers
One More Time (Coming soon)

How To Catch An Alpha
Catching Him
Baiting Him
Hooking Him

ABOUT ROCHELLE PAIGE

Rochelle absolutely adores reading—always has and always will. When she was growing up, her friends used to tease her when she would trail after them, trying to read and walk at the same time. If she has downtime, odds are you will find her reading or writing.

She is the mother of two wonderful sons who have inspired her to chase her dream of being an author. She wants them to learn from her that you can live your dream as long as you are willing to work for it.

OTHER BOOKS BY ROCHELLE PAIGE

BLYTHE COLLEGE SERIES
Push the Envelope
Hit the Wall
Summer Nights (novella duo)
Outside the Box
Winter Wedding (novella)

BACHELORETTE PARTY SERIES
Sucked Into Love
Checked Into Love
Mixed Into Love
Slapped Into Love
Married Into Love
Chased Into Love
Bounced Into Love

CRISIS SERIES
Identity Crisis
Protection Crisis

FATED MATES
Crying Wolf
Shoot for the Moo
Thrown to the Wolves
Bear the Consequences
Bear It All
Bear the Burden
Ask for the Moon
Bear Your Fate
The Empress

BODY & SOUL SERIES
Bare Your Soul
Save Your Soul
Sell Your Soul
Feed Your Soul
Body Language

FORTUITY DUET
Fortuity
Serenity

HAPPILY EVER ALPHA WORLD
Until Leo
Until Mani

STANDALONES
Star Pupil

Manufactured by Amazon.ca
Bolton, ON